Praise for the Cooked to Death Series

"A collection of exceptional and wildly compelling stories that set my teeth on edge. I was hooked from start to finish."

GERRY SCHMITT
New York Times best-selling author of the Afton Angler Thrillers

"These page-turning stories deliver chills as biting as a Minnesota winter. But in a good way. Scary, bizarre, and highly imaginative."

LAURA CHILDS
Award-winning author of the Cackleberry Club and
Scrapbooking Mysteries

"Tales of deception, deviousness, and infidelity with plenty of laughter sprinkled in for good measure pairs nicely with recipes that take your senses on a deep dive into the storytelling."

WILL SIMONS
Eater contributor and former Yelp community manager, Omaha

The Cooked to Death Series

Cooked to Death

VOLUME V

RESTAURANT IN PEACE

Edited by Rhonda Gilliland

COOKED TO DEATH VOL. V: RESTAURANT IN PEACE

eISBN: 978-1-7320216-4-8
ISBN: 978-1-7320216-5-5

Printed in the United States of America
First Printing 2020

Cover design by Ryan Engesser
Illustrations by Bonnie Planque

Obscura Productions

*In memory of Tommy Johnson of The Whiskey Sournotes,
best musician, friend, and soulmate.*

1958–2011

*A portion of the proceeds go to
the Minnesota Farmer's Market Association.*

RESTAURANT MENU

SOUP

RECIPES

PREFACE

"DID YOU EVER have an out-of-state guest who was in total shock that they were getting a decent meal in Minnesota?" This was a question posed to an audience at a Cooked to Death panel. Wendy Webb, author, pipes in, "I was just having that same conversation with someone the other day." New York City, Chicago, Los Angeles, Dallas, Denver, and, yes, the Twin Cities are food havens. I wanted people to be aware of the culinary scene in Minnesota.

I have been a foodie since I was a teenager, before there was even a word for it. Moving to the Midwest really honed the craft. So much so that it led to becoming a Yelp reviewer, and I have been a black elite for more than ten years. I'm even dubbed the Yelp Queen with over 1,500 reviews.

I wanted *Restaurant in Peace* to have a restaurant edge and to feature recipes exclusively from restaurants. Many local chefs were thrilled to be part of the project. Like everyone else, I have my favorites. Half my career was working in restaurants. The upcoming Charlie Awards, which is the Twin Cities culinary Academy Awards for chefs, restaurants, and food trucks, and *Minnesota Monthly*'s Food and Wine Experience in the spring remind me that I am in the right place, at the right time.

RHONDA GILLILAND, EDITOR

MURDER LEAVES AN AFTERTASTE

By Renée Valois

"I THOUGHT THIS was your favorite restaurant."

Yvonne Mullin sighed. "It is."

"So why are you spending more time playing with your food than eating it?"

"Amber Loughlin."

Her husband leaned toward her over his empty plate. "The little girl?"

"Yeah. I keep her photo propped on my desk, and I look at it every day. More than once. And I keep seeing the devastated faces of her parents when her body was found. But every suspect has an alibi—so far."

"What?"

"I know you don't believe in intuition."

Her husband smiled. "I'm starting to, being married to you."

"One of the guys I interviewed . . . I'm dying to get a search warrant, but I have no legitimate reason to give the judge. But there's something about him. His manner. Something feels off. My gut says he could be the guy." She grimaced. "But I need evidence."

"It's been over a year."

"That also bothers me." She threw her fork down. "This case is becoming way too cold!"

When people at nearby tables turned to stare at them, she lowered her voice. "Especially when it comes to Amber. She deserves resolution. She deserves justice. So do her parents."

2

"The DNA hasn't helped?"

"It matches precisely NO ONE in the database!"

The owner of the Italian restaurant hurried over with a card in his hand. "We are opening a new location in Saint Paul," he said. "You have been such wonderful regulars that I would like to invite you to the grand opening."

Yvonne got the impression that he was simply trying to calm her down, to distract her from whatever was causing her outburst. But she took the card. She stared at it for a moment.

Suddenly her appetite returned.

· · · · ·

Russell Kray smirked as he perused his favorite child porn site on his burner phone wearing disposable vinyl gloves. He bought the gloves in boxes of fifty, cheap insurance that the cops would never get his fingerprints even if they found the phone tossed into a pond or the Mississippi. They'd never find a way to tie him to his vices. He was too smart, and they were too dumb.

He hadn't yet posted anything starring Amber. He liked to wait a while after a kid's death, when the commotion had died down a bit.

She had been an especially pretty little tart, with her blonde curls; big, innocent eyes; and slight body. He had enjoyed pounding her, especially when she screamed so loud. Apparently, she hadn't liked the "gift" "Santa" had promised her.

He chuckled at the idea that the fat belly that repulsed adult women was such an attractant to little girls when paired with his bushy white beard. It made it easier to lure them to "Santa's workshop" to see what wonders he had in store for them.

He would love to post a video of Santa having his way with a little girl, except that was too dangerous. Even if they didn't see his face in the video, he couldn't risk giving away his body type or the fact that he had a "Santa" beard.

He had gotten away with his pleasures for over thirty years because of his caution, and he wasn't going to get caught. Ever. Years of more girls lay before him. He grinned at the thought, even as his arousal swelled, watching the toddler in the online video; the unknown child seemed more confused than scared.

He liked it when his girls got frightened. When they realized that something had gone terribly wrong. That Santa was evil, not good.

He was already keeping an eye on his chosen next victim, carefully scoping out her family's movements, habits, calendar, timing, and daycare.

She was a little redhead named Shannon who often wore her hair in braids. She went to ballet class every Wednesday after school. Her mom or dad dropped her off—and often arrived late to pick her up when class was over. Sometimes she stood outside in the dark waiting for them.

In a month or two, he'd make his move.

After he was satisfied, he took a drive to the river and tossed the phone. He'd already gotten his money's worth out of it. Cheaper than a whore. He bought the phones in bulk online, just like the gloves. Using stolen credit information.

Pulling into his driveway, he stopped the car by his mailbox and pulled the emergency brake so the vehicle wouldn't roll down the hill into the street. There wasn't much in the box. A bill, a lot of junk mail, an oversized coupon with a gorgeous photo of an Italian meal that said, "Free Dinner to our Neighbors! Grand Opening! Stop by and give us a try."

He loved to eat. It was second only to his favorite vice: little girls.

He scrutinized the photo. It was maybe the most beautiful plate of food he'd ever seen. And the deal details were perfect—free meal, no obligation to do anything, no sales pitch, no need to tip the waiters. The owners just wanted the neighbors to find out what a great new restaurant it was. Presumably they were confident everyone would be so delighted they'd come back.

Huh.

He got back in his car and drove into the garage. He had nothing planned for dinner that night. Why not?

• • • • •

The host at Bellissimo was gregarious, which annoyed Russell.

"Ah, you got our promotional postcard—excellent! I didn't think it would arrive so quickly."

Russell looked around the chic dining room. It was only half full, which surprised him, given the wonderful deal. "Maybe I was one of the first ones to receive it?" he said.

"Probably," agreed the host. "But it's good for another month, so people may just be waiting for a night that's better for them. I expect we'll be overwhelmed with diners the week it expires."

The host grabbed a menu and told Russell to follow him.

"I would rather sit toward the back," Russell said, after the host tried to seat him by the front window. It was darker there, and he preferred that.

The waiter who approached his table was a thin young man with a slight accent. Was it really Italian? Russell wondered. Or was the guy just faking it to provide "authentic" color to the joint?

The waiter told him that the meal was five courses, which would arrive in succession. He could choose from two options for each course. He could also enjoy a glass of wine, gratis. The waiter handed the five-course dinner menu and the liquor list to Russell, who settled back with a happy sigh.

He was glad that the menu didn't list calorie counts by the food items. He hated restaurants that did that. He wanted to eat what he wanted without anyone trying to shame him into making a "healthier" choice.

He refused to feel guilt or shame for anything he did.

The wine the waiter brought was very good—not a wine he would have expected as a freebie. The lovely red reminded him of blood. He had always loved the color of blood.

The minestrone soup was also good, as was the salad. The bruschetta was even better. For his main course, he chose the family's supposedly unbeatable Italian spaghetti with huge, savory meatballs—the menu claimed the recipe was brought over when the family came to America.

He was a spaghetti connoisseur, so he was skeptical of the claims, but would be happy to be proven wrong.

When a young woman brought his entrée, she said, "No offense, but you actually remind me of Santa Claus. Have you ever thought of being a store Santa? I understand they can make a ton of money."

"Yeah, I actually was Santa at a mall for one season. That was enough. I couldn't take all the tykes peeing on me."

She giggled.

Russell had originally thought posing as Santa would be a good way to scope out future victims. There were so many little girls! But he kept getting aroused when they sat on his lap, and he couldn't afford for some parent to notice that.

Plus, if he preyed on more than one of the kids, the dicks might find a universal connection with the jolly guy the girls had all met. So he scrapped being a mall Santa for playing each girl's personal Santa.

"What did you think of the spaghetti?" his waiter asked when he had finished the last bite.

"It's in my top three," said Russell. "I'm not sure it's number one—but I'd come back for it."

"That's what we want to hear," said the waiter with a smile. Soon he was back with a very decadent tiramisu.

It was the perfect finish to a wonderful meal. Russell would definitely return—even though he would have to pay next time. And he told the waiter that when he got up to leave.

He had not had a more pleasurable time since he did the last little girl.

· · · · ·

Yvonne was unhappy to learn that he was sitting right outside the swinging kitchen door, which had a small window near the top.

"We tried," said the waiter, "but he wanted to sit at the back."

"I get it," said Yvonne. "He probably doesn't want to be seen any more than I do."

When the waiter brought his empty soup bowl back into the

kitchen, Yvonne carefully plucked out the licked-clean spoon with gloves and slipped it into a bag. She did the same with the fork from his salad and the silverware from his entrée. She was especially happy to get the wine goblet and the glass that had held his water. She felt there would be plenty of residue on those.

She hid quietly in the back of the kitchen until the staff in front confirmed that Mr. Kray had driven away.

She thanked them profusely for their help and headed to her car.

• • • • •

When Russell answered the door, he felt a chill to see that bitch cop on the doorstep.

"Russell Kray," she said. "You're under arrest."

He almost slammed the door in her face. But there were two other cops behind the bitch and that might not go so well.

"On what charge?" he said, outraged. They couldn't possibly have anything to tie him to anything.

"The rape and murder of Amber Loughlin."

"I had nothing to do with that! I was never anywhere near the kid!"

The officer smiled like ice. "Your DNA says otherwise."

A sudden shock of fear went through Russell Kray. "That's impossible," he said. "No. No. Not possible." He didn't think he'd left any bodily fluids at the crime scene, and he was sure his DNA wasn't in the system. "No," he said.

"Yes," said Officer Mullin.

• • • • •

Amber Loughlin eventually got her justice. As did twelve other girls Kray had raped and murdered over the years, one every few years. There may have been more.

"The Santa Murderer" made the headlines as one of the most horrific serial killers ever. He hung himself when he was sentenced to life.

"I think he knew the other inmates would do terrible things to him when he landed in prison," said Yvonne's husband. "So he took the easy way out."

"My intuition says otherwise," Yvonne said.

"Oh?"

"He won't find Hell easy at all."

ANTONIO'S GENUINE ITALIAN SPAGHETTI SAUCE

Recipe from Antonio Turitto's restaurant, Naples, Italy (this is an old recipe that has been handed down in my family; the restaurant may no longer exist)

Makes 2 gallons

Ingredients

5 large cans tomato puree

4 large cans hot water

4 small cans tomato paste

2 small cans tomato sauce

2 tablespoons parsley flakes

1 tablespoon oregano flakes

1½ teaspoons salt

½ teaspoon black pepper

1 teaspoon red pepper powder (cayenne)

1 teaspoon garlic salt

1 teaspoon onion salt

1 tablespoon anise juice

½ cup fried, cut-up small onion

¼ cup fried, cut-up small green pepper

3 tablespoons sweet basil flakes

1 ounce garlic juice

1 cup Kraft cooking oil

3 tablespoons olive oil

GENUINE ITALIAN ROMONO MEATBALLS

Makes 24 large meatballs

Ingredients

3 pounds ground beef

2 pounds ground pork

½ teaspoon salt

¼ teaspoon black pepper

½ teaspoon red pepper powder

2 teaspoons garlic salt

1 tablespoon garlic juice

2 teaspoons onion salt

1½ cups cut-up small onion

¼ cup cut-up small green pepper

1 teaspoon anise juice

1 tablespoon oregano flakes

2 tablespoons parsley flakes

2 tablespoons sweet basil flakes

3 eggs

Directions

Mix the spaghetti sauce ingredients well.

Make meatballs about the size of a small apple. Roll balls firm and fry in 1 inch of hot oil until brown on all sides.

Put meatballs and pepperoni (optional addition) in large pan with spaghetti sauce and cook slowly, simmering for about 4 hours. Stir about every 15 minutes, until done.

IT'S IN THE BLOOD

By Rhonda Gilliland

THE IDEA OF marrying a non-Greek was equivalent to marrying someone who beat me. But being third-generation Greek-American, this trend was unavoidable. Another unavoidable trend was third generations running family restaurants into the ground. In the Tri-City area, there were so many Italian restaurants. A particular one, in Albany, New York, was the place to see and be seen every Friday and Saturday night. Our family had the only Greek restaurant around. It was started by my parents, George and Mary Theros. My brother Steve (Stefanos) and I worked there during the summer. My main priority in high school was running home after class so I could watch *Dark Shadows*. I wanted nothing to do with the business. Steve was being groomed for it. My parents wanted me to go to college. When I told my father I wasn't sure if that's what I wanted, he threatened to kill himself. All my friends from high school were studying to be nurses, so I got on the bandwagon and enrolled in nursing school.

I took a part-time job as a unit clerk in the ICU. In intensive care, you see the worst of the worst. The only thing I cared about was that it was air-conditioned. The late 1970s was also the prime of disco. So every weekend my friends and I would go to Sneaky Pete's in Latham. That's where I spotted the most gorgeous guy. He danced like John Travolta's teacher. I couldn't take my eyes off of him. I managed to get a seat at the bar and was drinking my sloe gin fizz, when I noticed the guy alongside me giving me the eye.

I asked him, "Don't you dance?"

He replied, "I dance in bed."

I laughed so hard I almost fell off my chair. That's when I knew Tom Johnson was the one.

He was from Minnesota, a student at SUNY Albany majoring in accounting who was moving back to the Twin Cities after graduation to join his father's accounting firm. I immediately changed my major to art and transferred to SUNY, but I still lived at home (although, I would spend many hours at the Dutch Quad with Tom). We were both very busy in school and decided to be discreet when it came to my family. Until that Christmas when he gave me a one-karat diamond engagement ring. I didn't know he had that kind of money. My family did very well and had the ultimate status symbol: a house on Manning Boulevard.

On spring break, he invited me to Minnesota to meet his family. It was my first time on a plane. His parents immediately took us to W.A. Frost for dinner. I'd never seen anything like the beauty and architecture of Saint Paul. Then we drove to their home on Summit Avenue, and my jaw dropped. The mansions made the houses on Manning Boulevard look like shacks! My whole stereotype of the Midwest changed in an instant. When you live out East, your whole mentality of the country is East Coast, West Coast, and Florida. Everything else is one big hick town. This was more progressive than anything I'd ever seen.

When I announced our engagement to my family and that I'd be leaving the state, the one who gave me the most grief was my brother, Steve. Surprisingly, my parents were starting to tire of the restaurant business. I sensed they were growing apart and were just married to the restaurant. I knew my father would rather deal with the grill than my mother most of the time. When they got an offer to sell the restaurant to someone who wanted to put in a juice bar, they jumped at it. They could see that all the great Italian restaurants, sub shops, and bakeries were all closing up. Dino's Greek would be one of the last. Sure enough, they decided to move to Florida. I assured them I would marry in the church and that our children would be raised Greek Orthodox, and they happily headed south.

After May graduation, we had an August wedding. We honeymooned in Grand Marais on the North Shore in northern Minnesota. We stayed at the East Bay Suites in a suite facing Lake Superior and World's Best Doughnuts. It was also the weekend of the Fisherman's Picnic, where all kinds of vendors lined Main Street. At night it was so romantic; hearing the waves crashing reminded me of the ocean.

· · · · ·

Tom and I lived in a large duplex that belonged to his grandparents. I had to get used to not calling it a flat. Like calling soda, pop. The documentary *How to Talk Minnesotan* is the truth. Tom was making good money in the family business, and it wasn't long before I was dreaming of a house on Summit Avenue. We had already joined the University Club. I still didn't know what I wanted as a career. I knew I wanted to be a mother, and I had wanted a son named Zack since I was twelve. I found a wonderful Greek Orthodox Church on Summit Avenue just five minutes away from our house. When I first joined, I felt self-conscious that I didn't have a Greek surname. Much to my shock many of the members had intermarried and I fit right in.

No one batted an eye when I gave birth to blond-haired, blue-eyed Zacharias. I invited my brother to be his godfather. I suggested Steve stay with us for a couple of weeks. During his visit, we took him to one of the Greek restaurants. A couple of bites into his gyros, he said, "I can't eat this." Steve was used to the Greek street food we were raised on.

We stopped at an Irish pub called the Dubliner on Lake Street in Minneapolis. One of our favorite Irish performers, Paddy O'Brien, was playing with his band. When Steve saw auburn-haired, green-eyed Irish beauty Jessica Laine, it was love at first sight for both of them. She was a middle school music teacher rooted in Saint Paul and wasn't going anywhere else. My brother never went back home. However, he insisted on an Orthodox wedding. That was the compromise. My parents flew in and left after a week. They were in total shock that they had a decent meal in Minnesota. Another stereotype of visitors.

Jessica actually ended up converting to the Greek Orthodox faith. I was her godmother, and a couple of years later, Jessica was godmother to our daughter Zoe, which means "life." Miraculously, the baby looked like me, black hair and brown eyes. A rarity in Minnesota. Jessica was unable to have children, so she relished her new role and took Zoe to communion every Sunday. Tom convinced his father to invest in a restaurant for Steve and he would do the books. I designed the menu. Lars, my father-in-law, insisted that it be a rented space. That way if the restaurant didn't make it, we weren't stuck with a building.

In spite of the high Grand Avenue rents, The Crazy Greek turned a profit in three years. People not only flocked there for the unique Greek flavors, but the best live music around. A lot of it Irish, which the neighborhood loved. We were able to buy the house on Summit Avenue, which we dubbed the Johnson Mansion. Why did I get an eerie feeling over how perfect this was?

· · · · ·

For the last six months, Tom was having an affair with the company receptionist and had decided to do some fancy bookkeeping so they could run off to South America. The way I found out was one day as I got home from shopping and pulled into the driveway, a guy jumped into the passenger side of my car and pointed a gun to my head. All I could think about at that moment was that I was so glad the kids were at Jessica's and that there would be blood all over the nicest car I ever owned. Tom had been so arrogant that he instructed his hitman, a meth head named Justin, to tell me that he wanted me out of the way permanently. That greedy pig!

I yelled, "Wait!"

When Justin went to collect his final payment, and the transaction was completed, Tom's smile changed to shock when he saw the gun pointed at him. "Your wife gave me $10,000 to kill you too. I like a woman who thinks of revenge, even facing her own death. In fact, I'm so impressed with her I'm gonna throw in your whore for free."

Tom and I were buried in a Greek cemetery together. Even the funeral parlor was on Summit.

There is a happy ending. Steve and Jessica moved into our Summit

Avenue house and raised Zack and Zoe. Jessica became pregnant after years of infertility issues. Baby Sylvia was born on my birthday. They named her after me. How about that?

And the restaurant? It's still thriving. It's in the blood.

KOTOPOULO LEMONATO/RIGANATO WITH POTATOES

Recipe from The Naughty Greek *by Angelo Giovanis*

Ingredients

Potatoes:

6 medium potatoes

4 soup spoons of olive oil

Pepper and salt to taste

Fresh thyme

Chicken:

One whole chicken, cut in 8 pieces

Marinade:

4 cloves garlic

1 cube of chicken stock

1 teaspoon oregano

2 lemons—zests and the lemon juice

50 grams olive oil

200 grams water

Fresh thyme

4 grams honey

60 grams yellow mustard

Execution Method: Preheat the oven to 400° F.

Directions for potatoes:

Cut the potato in length wedges.

Put a frying pan over a strong fire and add olive oil.

Once warmed, pour the potatoes and sauté them until they get color.

Add pepper, salt, and thyme fresh.

Mix until golden color.

When ready, transfer potatoes to an aluminum foil deep half pan.

Directions for the marinade: In a blender put the garlic, the chicken cube bouillon, the dry oregano, the zest and the juice of two lemons, extra virgin olive oil, water, lots of thyme, honey, and mustard. Beat on soft until the garlic dissolves and the ingredients blend well together.

Directions for the chicken:

Put the chicken in a bowl.

Pour marinade from above over the chicken.

Massage the chicken so that the marinade goes everywhere. You can cook it immediately or keep it for up to 1½ days in the refrigerator. The longer you leave it in the marinade, the more delicious it will be.

Place the chicken over the potatoes in the aluminum foil deep half pan.

Pour as much of the marinade as you can over the chicken.

Cover with aluminum foil.

Bake for 45 minutes with aluminum foil and for another 30–45 minutes without foil. Be sure to pour more marinade over the chicken while it is baking.

Plate: Place the potatoes on the plate first. Then add the chicken on top of the potatoes. Add a spoon of strained Greek yogurt. Season with the juices from the oven. Finish off with oregano and fresh thyme.

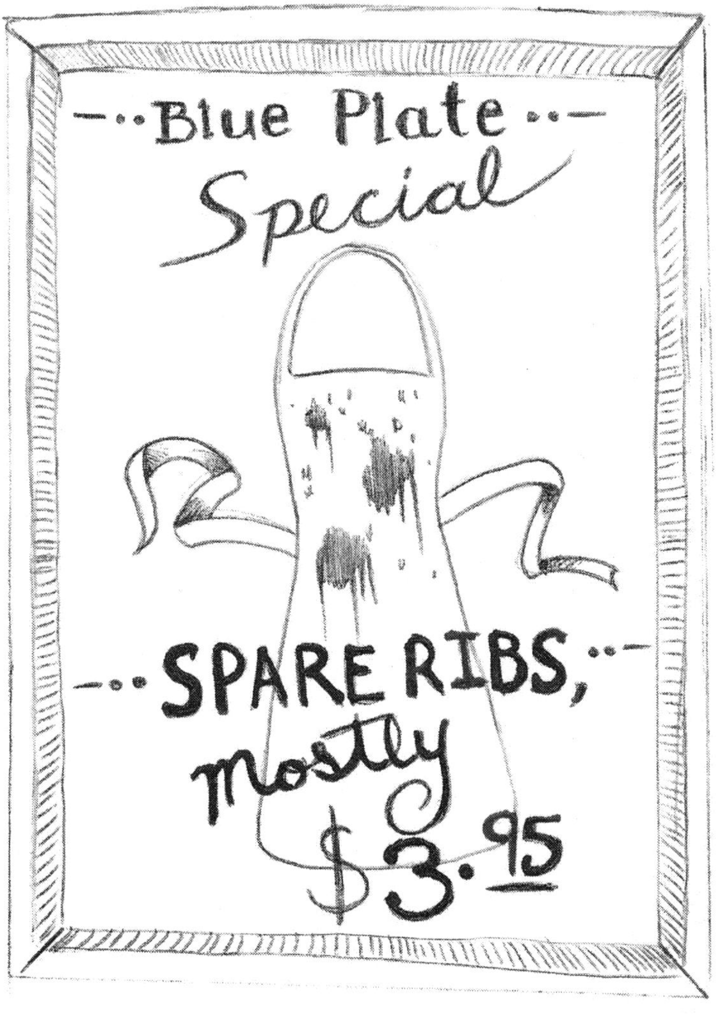
Blue Plate
Special
SPARE RIBS,
mostly
$3.95

PICKUP ARTIST

A TORY BAUER STORY

By Kathleen Taylor

"TACOMA."

"Come again?"

"I said, 'Tacoma.'"

"That's her legal name? Tacoma?"

"How the hell should I know? I ain't seen her birth certificate."

"Tacoma, like the truck?"

I leaned over the table, silently topping off their coffees as the Old Farts sat at their usual window booth and discussed the new bartender at Jackson's Hole across the street from the café. One or two acknowledged the refill, but mostly I was invisible to them.

"If she's bartending, she's not named after the truck. It hasn't been around that long."

"Since '95, it has." Bean paused for a second and squinted at the ceiling while he calculated, then nodded. "She could be old enough." He was the resident automotive expert.

"She don't look *that* young." That was Harold, expert in nothing, but firm in his opinions.

"Have you *seen* her?" Bean again.

"Well, no, but George did."

George was conveniently absent, therefore unable to confirm or deny.

"I heard . . ." said another.

They all leaned forward a bit and whispered, peeking over their shoulders to see if anyone was listening. I deliberately looked away. They'd finished breakfast but were nowhere near done hashing over the newcomer. Delphi newbies were fair game and always a hot topic.

The Old Farts were mostly retired farmers who had nothing else to do with their day but bitch and moan and argue about the weather and politics and each other.

I didn't need to overhear whatever else they were saying about the Mystery Barkeep. I could pretty well guess their secret speculations anyway. I was not about to mention that there was also a city named Tacoma, or the possibility that this fascinating new person could be named (legally or otherwise) after a town rather than a pickup. I just set their tickets in a pile, knowing that I'd be lucky to get a dollar tip out of the whole table.

Back at the Bunn, I rolled my eyes at Del, who was territorially intrigued with the newbie too, even though Del was officially out of circulation owing to a recent switch to celibacy which had lasted far longer than anyone expected (there was a pool). Just because she wasn't currently interested, didn't mean that she'd given up ownership of the town's collective male attention.

"What do you hear about her?" she asked me.

"Nothing more than what they're saying," I said, tilting my head Old Fart-ward. "And I don't think they know what they're talking about either. She's new, she works at the bar, she's young or maybe not so young, and she might be named after a truck or something. Beyond that, I got nuthin'."

"You're no help," Del muttered. She picked up a couple of Number 2 Specials from the counter, pasted a tight smile on her face, and headed over to a corner booth with the plates.

Celibate Del was cranky, though non-celibate Del was cranky too. She was my late husband's first cousin, and since we shared a single-wide trailer at the edge of Delphi, I was used to her moods. I just shrugged and continued with the usual morning shift routine—take the order, bring the coffee, pretend to agree with (or politely ignore) political opinions, serve the food, wonder why Aphrodite Ferguson left the café to me when I was perfectly content being a waitress and leaving the job at the job at the end of my shift.

Unfortunately, when you own the café, there's no "leaving the job at the job." It's with you. Always.

You know, same-old same-old.

Except that there was someone new in town.

And everyone was intrigued.

"Well, I heard her name was Camry," Neil Pascoe said. We were sitting in his kitchen, a floor above the library that he ran out of his house. He was stir-frying shrimp and garlic. Small-town café food was café food, edible, filling and fattening, but not notable. Once a week or so, Neil cooked for me. It smelled delicious, and I was starving

"The automotive rumor mill needs to get its poop in a group," I said. "They're going to run out of vehicle names pretty soon."

"Mercedes," Neil said, popping a shrimp into his mouth.

"Denali," I said.

"Tundra," we both said together, laughing.

"So, you wanna go take a peek at Mini Cooper in the flesh, Tory?"

"You mean, go to the bar? Now? On a Tuesday?"

"Unless you can figure out a way to get her to come to the library tonight," he said. "I, myself, am curious to find out which vehicle she's actually named after."

It had been a long day. Tomorrow would be a long day, and I was due to open at 5:00 a.m. I was tired, and I had the new Stephen King that Neil had set aside for me. Home was just across the street with Del and her son, Presley. I'd been looking forward to putting on my jammies and climbing into bed to read directly after supper. And then I remembered that Pres had lately taken up the tuba. He played with an enthusiasm only a thirteen-year-old boy could muster.

"Yes," I said.

South Dakota's eating/drinking establishments have been smoke-free for a long time, but the ghost whiff of smoke still lingers in the old, dark wood of Jackson's Hole. It greets you at the door, and I swear it gets into your clothes and makes your eyes burn even now. I rubbed my eyes as they adjusted to the interior darkness.

For a Tuesday night, the place *was* hopping. Most of the tables were full, and even the Old Farts were there, minus George, at a table in the far corner.

"Looks like we're not the only ones curious," Neil said, bringing our drinks—Black Russian for me and a beer with olives for him—to the table.

"So where is she?" I had already scoped the place out, absently noting who would turn up at the café in the morning, hungover. I recognized every single person there, including Pat, the bar's co-owner. Generally dour, she was smiling broadly, lighting up at each sale.

The mystery newbie was a cash cow.

"Haven't spotted her yet, but I did hear a plausible name, though," Neil said. "Lexie."

"That's not a car," I pointed out.

"But it's like *Lexus*," he said, "and you know how things travel here. Someone repeated it wrong, someone heard them wrong, someone else forgot everything but *like a car name*." He spread his hands out and shrugged. "Voilà."

"You get that from Pat?" I asked him.

"She was too busy for chit-chat. I got it from over there." He pointed in the direction of the Old Farts. "George was their go-to for info, I guess."

"Oh. Well, in that case, I'm still sticking with Denali. Stopped clocks are right more often than that bunch." I looked down, surprised to find that my glass was empty. I stood up and said, "I'll get the next round."

I caught Pat's eye at the bar and signaled for more, then headed down the hallway to the bathroom.

A couple of laughing girls came in after me, and from inside my stall, I could hear their slurry conversation.

"It's crazy out there. Never seen it like this on a Tuesday."

"You know why. Everyone wants to see *her*."

"Ugh. Who cares? Anyone who moves to this dump can't be very special. Or smart."

"Tell that to Hunter. He said he was coming uptown tonight with or without me. I figured I'd better come too. He says she's totally hot."

"So, is she?"

"No clue. I haven't seen her yet."

"Bitch," one said.

"Bitch," the other agreed. And they both left the bathroom.

At the bar, waiting for Pat to finish putting up our drinks, I realized the bathroom girls were right. I had never seen the bar this busy on a weeknight, especially when nothing was happening in town—no big sports games, no holiday parties, no karaoke.

Thank goodness.

I looked around the bustling bar. While most of the drinkers picked up their own drinks and paid at the till, there were a couple of servers trucking trays around the room. I knew both of them.

The bar was dark, but there was still enough light to be certain that there were no strangers among the natives. And it was light enough to see that I wasn't the only one surreptitiously checking everyone else out.

We all wanted a peek at the new person.

Pat set our drinks in front of me. I fished tip bills and change from a jeans pocket. As she rang up the total, I asked, "So where is your new-bie? Everyone is real curious about her." Pat grinned. It was an unusual expression for her, and I don't think her face liked it. The result was kind of frightening. "I sent her to the back room for more Kahlua," she said, pointing at my Black Russian. "She'll be out in a minute." Pat turned away abruptly to take another order.

I watched her back for a second, shrugged, and picked up the drinks.

"So?" Neil asked. It was both a question and a statement. "Saw you talking to Pat. Did you at least figure out her name?"

Dammit, I knew I'd forgotten something. "No, but Pat says she's in the back room and will be out soon."

So we drank our drinks, and someone sent over another round to us, and we drank them. And one way or another, in and among the laughter and greetings of neighbors and the rehashing of old news that comprises every visit in a small-town bar, I never made it back to the bar to ask Pat the all-important question.

We waited as long as we could manage, but Denali never did make an appearance. Maybe she'd been sent to the Sioux Falls for that Kahlua. Morning was approaching a lot faster than I wanted it to, and I'd had at least one more drink than I actually needed.

"Tundra's been good for business," Neil said, as we stood up to leave. "Pat might actually keep smiling."

I doubted that, but Neil's comment triggered a thought.

On our way to the door, I stopped here and there, and asked each person I talked to, the same two questions.

Each person gave me the same two answers.

I opened the next morning, bleary and a little headachy and nowhere near rested. I'd just turned the coffee on when George ambled in.

I brought his usual over to the Old Fart's booth and slid in across from him.

"George," I said, trying a smile and failing. Smiling made my eyes hurt. "Just the person I wanted to see."

"Uh-oh," he said, stirring his coffee even though he had not added any sugar or creamer. "What did I do now?"

"Nothing. Not a thing," I said, letting the grin go. It probably unsettled him. "I just want to ask you about the new waitress over at Jackson's."

He blew on his cup and took a sip. "Why the hell does everyone think I know anything about her?"

"Everyone?"

"You're the third person to ask me." He shook his head, bewildered.

"Harold said that you'd seen her. I mean, like, actually seen her in person."

And every person I'd asked the previous evening invoked George as a source. That had been one of my questions.

"Harold," George said, raising an eyebrow at me and repeating, "Harold."

I got his meaning.

"Yeah," I said, shaking my head at my own silliness. "I should have known better. Tell you what, your breakfast is on me this morning. That make up for bugging you?"

He grinned. "You can bug me any time, Tory."

Halfway to the counter, I stopped, turned around, and asked George the other question I'd asked everyone the night before.

And I got the same answer.

I tried to suppress a smile, but it slipped out occasionally during the shift.

"What are you grinning about?" Del asked. She was still cranky, and it was not okay to be not-cranky when she was cranky.

"Nothing, I'm just in a good mood," I lied. "Let me know if you spot Pat pulling up at the bar, would ya?"

Del just shook her head and went about her shift. Around one, after the lunch rush had waned, she nodded toward the window.

Pat had just parked her truck in front of Jackson's Hole.

"Can you hold down the fort for a bit? I'll be right back," I said, not waiting for Del's reply.

"Not used to seeing you this time of day, Tory," Pat said as I walked into the bar. "Taking up day drinking?"

"Tempting," I said. And if I hadn't been mildly hungover, I might even have considered having a drink in the empty bar. "But no. I need you to settle a bet for me, if you can."

Pat, a little wary, "Ooookay."

"I think your new waitress is named Denali. How close am I?"

Pat relaxed and then laughed. "Sierra. Her name is Sierra."

And there it was—the vehicle connection.

"And when did she start working here?"

"Last week sometime," Pat said, not meeting my eyes.

"And since then, she's been working every day?"

"Yup." The smile was gone.

"Everyone's heard about her. Everyone's very curious. Most of us have popped in for a drink, hoping to get a peek at her. You've had quite the nightly crowds."

"It's been a good week," Pat agreed. "Word gets around pretty fast here, you know. We don't have much other entertainment."

I waited. Pat finally looked directly at me.

I smiled.

She smiled.

"I suppose *Sierra* will be quitting soon. Moving on to greener pastures," I said. "Might even leave suddenly, with no forwarding address or contact info."

Pat allowed as to how that was almost certainly possible.

Probable even.

"*Everyone* will be so sorry they didn't get to meet her," I said. And then I smiled again.

Not one person, no one, had actually seen her. Heard about her, yep. Talked about her, yep. Repeated erroneous names? Took Harold at his word about George's expertise? Yep and yep.

But no one I talked to had seen this vehicular paragon in person, including George. It was almost as if she never existed.

"Sure you don't want that drink, Tory? It's on the house."

"I'll take a raincheck," I said. "But thanks."

On the way back across the street to my own nearly empty business, I thought about the good week Pat had had at the bar, about the unusual crowds, and the windfall of cash.

And I wondered if I could announce a mystery server of my own.

And what I would name her.

THE FRENCH ONION BURGER

Recipe from Chef Mik German and Glen Wadie

FRENCH ONIONS

2 large yellow onions, julienne

1 tablespoon kosher salt

1 tablespoon minced garlic

2 teaspoons red pepper flake

2 teaspoons dry thyme

¼ cup extra virgin olive oil

Cook together in a sauté pan on medium heat. Allow the onions to soften and become translucent.

Deglaze your pan using ¼ cup Worcestershire.

1 tablespoon beef base (I prefer Better Than Bouillon, but a beef bouillon cube will also work)

2 bay leaves

2 cups chicken stock (I prefer Swanson)

Place all of the remaining ingredients into the stock pot, reduce liquid by half on medium heat.

FRENCH ONION BURGER MIX

1 pound 80/20 ground beef (use a local butcher, not the grocery store)

6 ounces shredded Swiss cheese

About half of your French onion mixture

Mix all of the ingredients together by hand, form into burger patties. I like a 6-ounce burger but follow your heart.

After you have cooked the burgers, top them with the remaining French onion mixture and Swiss cheese.

CHAMPAGNE WISHES AND CAVIAR DREAMS

By M.E. Bakos

"TODAY, I HAVE new chef! We go upscale!" Ivan announced, beaming.

"Da!" Maggie said. She smiled broadly and her bright blue eyes sparkled with excitement. Ivan and his wife, Maggie, a chubby, blonde woman notable for wearing bright red lipstick and high heels, routinely greeted customers at the front of Ivan's Bar and Grill. Although he and Maggie had lived and worked in the US many years, they still bore accents of their native Russia.

Myra and I were meeting for lunch to discuss my latest rehab project and catch up on our lives. Ivan's was our go-to restaurant in Crocus Heights, Minnesota. It was a comfortable, low-key restaurant that opened for lunch and dinner. Evenings, the grill turned into a modest nightclub where patrons could karaoke or dance to local bands. Nothing fancy.

"I stole chef from five-star restaurant!" Ivan bragged. "He was trained by the best chefs in a fabyeles (fabulous) cooking school." The grill seemed an odd career choice for an up-and-coming chef, but Ivan and Maggie always had staff changes. It wasn't unusual to see new employees.

"It is my Maggie's passion," Ivan beamed, his arm around his wife's waist. "We have the finest food!" She looked at Ivan, glowing with his compliment. Her lips were painted a brighter shade of red than I recalled. Her hair teased to greater heights.

I studied Maggie, who stood shorter than Ivan that day. "No heels, today, Maggie?" I asked.

"Nyet!" Maggie said, "I hurt foot," and pointed to her flats.

"I'm sure we'll enjoy the new menu," Myra said, agreeably. "Sorry about your injury."

I smiled at Ivan and Maggie. "Change is good," I said. Actually, I liked the restaurant as it was. The Ivan Burgers were to die for, and then there were the large glasses of wine. It was a luxury to visit with friends and kibitz uninterrupted. I wasn't a big fan of change.

We followed a new staffer, a maître 'd, who sported a black bow tie, starched shirt, and dress pants.

"Are we really at Ivan's?" I whispered to Myra.

"It'll be a nice change, Katelyn," she murmured.

I had left work at my newest rehab in jeans and sweatshirt. Thank goodness, I wore a coat that hid my casual attire. Myra wore classic casual, black coat and slacks, her sweater adorned with a bright silk scarf. An outfit that could go anywhere. Her hair was perfect. We followed the host to a table covered with a white tablecloth and cloth napkins. The new host waited until we were seated, then smoothly handed us menus and recited the specials of the day.

"Would you look at all the dishes and flatware?" I whispered. In place of the usual coffee mug, there were cups and saucers, bread plates, wine and water glasses, along with five-piece silverware settings.

"Yes." Myra nodded and smiled. "It's lovely."

After taking our drink order, the host glided away. The door to the kitchen was propped open. From our booth, I could see supplies stacked on shelves. On the floor by boxes of napkins and paper towels were the faint outlines of footprints.

"You don't suppose we could ask for another table?" I stifled a snicker and gestured at the open door.

"You could ask, but that woman would probably throw us out," Myra pointed to Katarina with a wry smile. I snorted. Katarina was a touchy brunette, also Russian, who'd survived all the staff changes. She had never been very friendly and glared at us as she passed our booth.

"Why do you think she hates us?" I asked Myra in a low voice.

"I don't think it's personal," Myra said, in a hushed tone. Just then the sharp-voiced waitress reappeared, and we watched curiously as she trotted by, her dark hair tightly bound in a bun. She slammed a water pitcher on the table of an older couple and hustled off to the kitchen. The customers were startled and stopped talking, their mouths open.

"Yep, Myra, you're right. She's just cranky."

"Ivan runs a tight ship."

We opened the menu. I choked and asked, "What is this stuff?"

"It's not casual comfort food," Myra chuckled.

"It's not even close. Russian caviar? Pheasant and steamed clams? I want my Ivan Burger and fries."

"They still have wild rice soup," Myra suggested. "Maybe the Swedish meatballs?"

"Have you seen the prices?" I asked and gulped.

"My treat. Let's try it." She smiled. "Fine dining in Crocus Heights is a rare event. It'll be fun. We're here. And, Ivan and Maggie would love to see their customers happy."

"All right," I agreed. "I just hope the food is good."

"I do too." Myra smiled and her hazel eyes twinkled. "How is the new rehab going?"

My new occupation as a house flipper could be challenging. Especially since each renovation seemed to come with a dead body. I hoped this one would be different. No dead bodies or bad karma. So far, so good.

"Great." I beamed. "I met a neigh . . ."

"Eeeek!" I looked to the open kitchen door and stood to investigate the scream, but Myra held me back. Katarina ran from the kitchen. Ivan hurried from the front desk and dashed to the kitchen.

"What is problem?" Ivan yelled.

"In the walk-in refrigerator! The busboy is dead!" A deep brogue answered. "Call 9-1-1!"

Myra and I gasped, and we stared at each other.

"That must be the new chef," I whispered. "Sounds like he could be an Aussie?"

"Yes." She nodded. We waited for what seemed to be an eternity while customers around us huffed and strained to view the commotion.

Police officers and ambulance personnel flooded the restaurant.

One officer closed the restaurant, while another took customer's contact information. We sighed with relief after giving our information and the cop said we were free to leave. One by one, diners got up and walked out of the restaurant.

We followed suit, hearing Ivan's voice, "It is terrible accident. A case of champagne fell on his head."

"The medical examiner will determine the cause of death," the officer responded.

"Katarina found him. She needed butter for the customers," the cook said loudly. "He must have been reaching for a carton and jostled the heavy crate in the process."

In the parking lot, an officer questioned Katarina. Her shoulders shook, and she covered her eyes in distress.

"She found the body. Standard procedure, interrogating the staff," I said.

"I'm sure," Myra agreed.

We parted ways. Myra went to her slick SUV. While heading to my latest economy car, a Ford Festiva, I glanced back at Katarina. From inside my car, I continued to watch the officer grill the woman until she parted her fingers enough to glare at me. The look chilled me to the bone. Gasping and startled, I started up the car and drove off.

At home, still shaken from Katarina's piercing gaze, I called Myra.

"Myra, you won't believe this, but I think Katarina was putting on an act for the police!'

"Katelyn, Why do you say that?"

"She gave me the stink eye!"

"While she was talking to the cop?" She sounded puzzled.

"Yes! She was quick. The officer was writing on his pad when she peeked out from her hands and gave me the evilest look, ever."

"The woman is a little touchy. She wasn't happy being interrogated and sensed someone was watching," she reasoned.

"I didn't see any tears."

"Oh. That *is* strange. When we left, her shoulders were shaking, as if she was crying," Myra said. "Let's go to Ivan's next week. Let the dust settle and keep our ears open for anything on the news."

"Sounds like a plan."

· · · · ·

A week later, we met at Ivan's for an early dinner. "Welcome back to fine dining!" Ivan greeted us with a wide grin.

"Da!" Maggie said. She beamed. Her eyes gleaming, her cheeks rosy with rouge.

The host seated us, recited the specials, and left us to ponder our choices. I sighed, opening the menu. I missed the pure comfort food: burgers, beef pot roast, chicken pot pie with flaky crust, meatloaf and mashed potatoes.

"Oh, look. There's Katarina." Myra looked over my shoulder at the next table.

I craned my head and saw Katarina drop dishes into a dishpan. She wore a white cap, starched shirt, black skirt, and apron as she bussed dishes. I heard a noise that sounded as if a plate or glass had broken with her handling. She hoisted the pan of dirty dishes and stomped to the kitchen.

"Looks like a demotion," Myra murmured. "I've never seen her buss dishes before. Must be part of the move to upscale, new chef and all."

"She should have been fired," I grumbled.

"She must be family," Myra said.

"Has to be," I agreed.

While we waited for the server to take our orders, I observed other customers look at their menus, put them aside, get up, and file out. After the third table of patrons left abruptly, we heard voices from the kitchen.

"No one wants to eat this sheeeet!" It was Katarina, in a high-pitched voice.

"Impossible! It is the finest cuisine!" the deep Aussie voice responded.

"Bah!" Katarina retorted.

Ivan obviously distraught, charged into the kitchen. "Customers walking out! We have to use old menus!" he yelled. "I go broke!"

"I do not cook hamburgers!" the chef yelled.

"You cook hamburgers, or I fire you!" Ivan yelled.

"Harrumph!"

"I can cook hamburgers," another voice piped up.

"Impossible! A mere dishwasher cannot cook!" the chef came back. "Not even a hamburger!" More sounds of dishes falling and breaking along with flatware hitting the floor.

"Time to go," I whispered.

"Good idea." We quietly walked out of the restaurant avoiding Maggie's gaze. She stood in her usual place at the front desk to greet customers, away from the fray. When she saw us leave, she headed to the kitchen.

Outside, we couldn't contain our mirth and spent a few minutes composing ourselves. Still hungry, I said, "There's the Northern Lake Tavern and Grill? I've heard good things."

"Sounds good. I'll meet you there," Myra responded.

Seated at a high-top table in the bustling restaurant, I marveled to Myra, "No drama. Just burgers, fries, and good food."

"That's true," she nodded appreciatively and grinned at me. "This could be our new favorite. I'd miss Ivan and Maggie though."

"I know," I groaned. "Maybe Ivan will see that he had the best of both worlds with awesome food, loyal clientele, great coffee, and good wine."

"Maybe. Why do you suppose he went along with the idea to go upscale?"

"Who knows? To please Maggie? Get snippy Katarina away from waiting on customers? Make a name for the restaurant?" I speculated.

"Maybe. Could be all of that. I'm curious to hear what the medical examiner says about the busboy. I wonder if a case of champagne really did fall on his head and kill him."

"I'm curious too." I nodded.

We didn't wait long. According to that evening's local news, the medical examiner ruled the cause of death was consistent with blunt force injury. The bottles of champagne had been scattered over him to disguise the fatal blow.

· · · · ·

Myra and I met at the Northern Lake Tavern again and kibitzed about the news.

"In all the fracas about the restaurant going to fine dining, the busboy's death has been forgotten," I said.

"Who do you suppose killed him?" she asked.

"It could have been the cook. He was in the kitchen when the busboy was found."

"That's true." She nodded.

"Maybe Katarina? She found the body. And, why would Katarina shed crocodile tears?" I remembered her evil eye.

"Hmm. I see your point," Myra said. "You think she did it?"

"Ivan demoted her to bussing tables. I think she had been a floor manager. Which is why we never crossed her," I added, chuckling.

"It could have been worse; Ivan could have made her dishwasher, Myra groaned.

"But, if she had done the deed, she wouldn't be working," I said, deflated. "She'd be in jail."

"True enough," Myra agreed.

"The cook could have done him in. He had opportunity," I countered.

"Yes. But, would he have kept cooking if he killed the busboy and the body was in the refrigerator?"

"Cooks are under a lot of pressure with customer orders. He could handle it," I said confidently.

"Maybe. He sounded distressed."

"Good actor," I said.

"Hmm."

I left Myra and went to my latest flip house and studied the worn kitchen refrigerator. Thoughts of the broken champagne bottles and the shoe prints left in the dust of the kitchen floor at Ivan's nagged at me. I made a few calls and headed to Ivan's Fine Dining.

Maggie and Ivan stood behind the counter.

I walked up to Maggie. "Maggie, you killed the busboy, didn't you?" Her face paled.

"Nyet!" She shook her teased blonde locks vigorously. Her blue eyes glittered.

"What you mean? My Maggie never kill nobody. You go!" Ivan roared and pointed to the exit.

"Yes, Maggie. You know you did!"

"Nyet!" She grabbed her coffee cup and threw it at me. I ducked. She came around the front counter and tackled me, screaming, "Busboy hate dishes! He go!" I twisted out of her meaty hands and found a chair leg, grabbed it, and threw the chair at her bulk, keeping her at bay.

"You crazy!" Ivan screamed, jumping up and down.

Just then, two officers entered and grabbed Maggie. They cuffed Maggie, read her rights, and hauled her to a waiting squad car.

"What is going on?" Ivan pleaded, following the officers to the car.

I dusted off while Myra joined me. "Thanks for coming." I caught my breath and straightened. "It's good to see a friendly face!"

"Did you call the cops on Maggie?"

"I did," I said, smoothing my hair. "The footprints to the kitchen resembled high heel prints. I'd never seen Maggie out of her high heels. That day, she had changed to flats. It was suspicious."

"Why Maggie?"

"The busboy complained about bussing more dishes with his job. Katarina hated the dishes too. Maggie didn't want anyone to get in the way of her dreams of fine dining. Fine dining meant more staff and more dishes. But Ivan was concerned about making money with fine dining. He didn't want the change as much as she did."

"How did she do it?" Myra asked.

"She waited until the restaurant closed, sent Ivan home, and surprised the busboy in the cooler. She clobbered him with a bottle of bubbly and dumped the case of champagne on him. He was always the last to leave because he did the evening kitchen cleanup. Maggie knew he wouldn't be found until the next day. Time of death would be difficult to determine in the walk-in frig. No one would suspect her because she stayed out front, in her stilettos, away from the kitchen."

"But, in the process of clobbering the busboy, her shoes were soaked," Myra guessed. "And, wearing different shoes would throw off the investigators."

"Yes!" I smoothed my pants. "What do you suppose Ivan will do now?"

"Close," Myra said firmly.

"Dang it. I hate it when a good restaurant closes."

"There's always the Northern Lake Tavern," Myra said, with a smile.

"Let's go!"

We sat at the table, happily munching Chimichurri steak sandwiches, when Myra stopped, her eyes wide. She pointed.

"What?" I followed her gesture. A sharp-faced, brunette stood up and left money on her table for the bill. "OMG. It's Katarina!" We stared while the woman zipped her purse and left.

"Well, a girl has gotta to eat," Myra said, a twinkle in her eye.

CHIMICHURRI STEAK SANDWICH

Recipes from Jessica Johnson, Northern Lake Tavern & Grill, Chisago City, Minnesota

Shaved ribeye cooked in cilantro garlic chimichurri sauce, topped with onion strings and swiss cheese, served on a toasted ciabatta roll.

CHIMICHURRI SAUCE

Ingredients

8 cups parsley, fresh, whole

8 cups cilantro, fresh, whole

4 tablespoons fresh squeezed lemon juice

½ cup garlic cloves

1 teaspoon kosher salt

1 teaspoon black pepper

2 cups olive oil

Directions

Put all ingredients, except oil, in Robot Coupe (a commercial food processor). Blend in the processor and gradually add oil. Put in container. Label.

TZATZIKI CHICKEN WRAP

Sliced chicken breast, house-made cucumber tzatziki sauce, tomato, red onion, cheddar cheese, and lettuce, served in a spinach wrap.

CUCUMBER TZATZIKI SAUCE

Ingredients

3 cucumbers, peeled, diced

3 cups sour cream

3 cups mayo

1½ teaspoons granulated garlic

4½ teaspoons dill, dried

1½ teaspoons kosher salt

1½ teaspoons black pepper

Directions

Mix all ingredients, but cucumber, in a large mixing bowl. Add cucumber and mash with whisk. Transfer to new container. Label.

MY BROTHER'S KEEPER

By Jason Lee Willis

IN THE HUMID stillness of an August night, the sound of a ceramic lid bouncing off the wooden planks of the kitchen floor ripped Bjorn Forsberg from his dreams and jolted him into a living nightmare.

He's in the house.

In Bjorn's mind, yellow teeth grinned maliciously in the darkness, even though a wall separated the bedroom from the kitchen. He tried swallowing, but fear stuck in his throat like a cold knife pressed under his chin.

Bjorn's foot searched under the cotton sheet until it made contact with his brother Gus, who also slept in the large bed. The sound of the lid of the cookie jar hitting the wooden plank had only made a single thud, but unlike the rest of the sleeping family, Bjorn understood what was happening.

He's here because of me.

A pine board groaned as the weight of a human body depressed it a quarter of an inch and then released it when stepping away. The friction of the nail within the loose board betrayed the location of the intruder. Bjorn knew that squeaky board.

Bjorn kicked Gus harder.

A sudden gasp filled the bedroom as Gus woke from the jarring kick. Bjorn held his breath and remained motionless on his side of the bed.

Do something, Bjorn pleaded in his mind.

The next sound did not come from the dark kitchen but from the barn, where Goliath, the big draft horse, stirred in his pen. He snorted, clearing his nostrils to identify the threats creeping around the barn. Hearing the subtle alarm, Gus gasped again and sat up in bed on his elbows to listen.

A crash of tin cups thundered through the kitchen, followed by the sound of the front door flying open with such force that it struck the wall, shaking the house.

Gus leapt for the corner of the bedroom and returned from the dark recesses with his prized fowling rifle clutched in his hands. Sitting on the side of the bed and staring uncertainly at the bedroom door, he held the gun ready across his chest.

The saddle horses in the barn whinnied in alarm, and the milking cows joined the chorus. The soft tremors of running feet echoed on the grassy yard, but Bjorn could not tell if they were coming or going.

Then a loud yawp pierced the night, followed by three or four other war cries.

"Injuns!" Gus said with full voice and jumped from bed.

Not Indians . . . something worse.

Gus stood at the window, fumbling at the latch before throwing aside the screen. His rifle muzzle searched the darkness for a target.

The adjacent wall shook, and his parents' bedroom door flew open and recoiled against the shared wall. Bjorn heard the unmistakable footsteps of his father charging through the kitchen in the dark and the sound of his mother's perfect kitchen again being disrupted.

A pistol blast shattered the night as his father stood at the doorway of the house, ready to defend his family from attack. In the distance, a half dozen Indian cries mocked the ineffectual shot as horses galloped off in the distance.

Lamplight soon filled the house and the yard, bringing a bit of security to the startled Forsberg family, all except Bjorn, who stood looking down at the lid of the cookie jar on the floor.

They knew right where to find it.

After a few minutes, Pa and Gus returned from a patrol of the outbuildings with a perplexing report.

"The gates and doors of the barn were all opened," Pa told Ma, waiting by the front door. "But they didn't take or kill anything."

"We must've stopped them before they could," Gus muttered, his eyes scanning the darkness.

"It'll be a few hours before dawn arrives, so we're going to have to hold tight until morning," Pa said. "Gustaf, Bjorn . . . light the rest of the lanterns. We'll set them outside so them damn Indians don't sneak up on us again. They didn't come all this way for nothing."

The boys went into motion and helped set out the six lanterns they owned fifty yards past the house to create an illuminated perimeter.

Pa, born Sigmund Forsberg in Sweden, was a wiry man of thirty-six, with short hair parted to one side and a bushy red beard that fanned out below his chin like a broom. With the yard illuminated, he maintained a stout defense. He carried a rifle and pistol, and then armed Gustaf with the deer rifle and Bjorn with the fowling gun. The three watched every shadow until the glow of the rising sun stole away every place for a renegade Indian to hide.

Ain't no Indians out there in the shadows, Bjorn told himself as they waited for the sun to peek over Jackson Lake.

It had been fifteen years since the last Indian attack in the area, when Gustaf was just a baby. Although the Sioux had been removed in 1862 to the Dakota territory, it did not stop a few renegade attacks from occurring in the following years, bringing the deaths of Noble Root and Squire Mack in the summer of 1864 and the massacre of the Jewett family the following year.

Bjorn had never so much as seen an Indian during his twelve years of life, but he'd read all about the Great Sioux War fought in the distant Black Hills, where General Custer had been killed. Since the surrender of Crazy Horse two years earlier, there were no longer news stories about Indian attacks, leaving Bjorn only short stories and novels to fill his imagination.

"Oh no, Sigmund!"

Both Pa and Gus rushed back inside, but Bjorn manned his post, already knowing about the cookie jar.

"They took the money," Ma explained. "The entire jar is missing. The lid dropped off, but they took the jar. It's gone, Sig, all gone!"

The mystery of the thieving Indians was slowly peeled away when

Pa returned outside and knelt down in a patch of dirt, now visible in the glow of the coming day. Bjorn maintained his spot on the opposite corner of the house, and Gus also stared at his father in curiosity.

The silence was broken by a loud and angry outburst from Pa, "The hell if it was Indians." Then he proceeded to kick a patch of dirt with the heel of his boot until he had to catch his breath. "Gustaf, go fetch my horse."

Gus obeyed and immediately jogged off toward the barn, but Ma followed Pa closely, demanding an explanation from the doorway. "Where are you going, Sig?"

"I'm not going to be made the fool!"

"What is that supposed to mean?"

"Somebody wanted me to think they were Indians. I'm going to get to the bottom of this."

"Sigmund! There were half a dozen of them. You're going to get yourself killed."

"Only if I'm wrong. I'll be back in twenty minutes. If I don't come back, Gustaf can ride to Shelbyville and raise an alarm."

Real Indians would have stolen the horses instead of the money, Bjorn agreed, feeling the knot in his belly tighten even more.

Gus brought Pa's finest saddle horse, Dala, across the yard. Pa handed Ma his rifle before hopping up on the horse and riding straight west toward the Blue Earth River.

It was the longest twenty minutes of Bjorn's life.

Ma, standing outside in the dim light of dawn, began to cry, but just as soon as she began, she wiped her face and continued to stare out to the west. The Blue Earth River valley stretched from Blue Earth City near the Iowa border all the way to Mankato. Narrow and deep, it protected the folks of Shelbyville, and the rest of the county, from wildfires that typically came on west winds.

"Oh, sweet Jesus," Ma finally said as a dark figure appeared on the horizon.

It was Pa, riding hard.

Dala came galloping into the yard, kicking up dirt and dust as she stopped in front of the house. Pa did not dismount. "Just as I thought. They weren't Indians."

"Not Indians?" Ma asked. "Then who broke into our house?"

"Those sons of bitches from Shelbyville. They know. Somehow, they found out what was happening tonight. I rode down to the river, knowing they'd have to cross there, and in the soft mud, I saw hoof prints from the horses, with the distinct markings of a horseshoe forged from Eli Hoffman's smithy. How would any Injun know we stashed away a hundred dollars in a cookie jar above the stove? Somehow they knew. I'm going to see if Widow Brush and the Brace family had the same thing happen to them."

Ma wasn't having any of his heroism. "You need to get the sheriff. They stole months worth of savings."

"I need to make sure other folks *don't* go to the sheriff claiming to see Indians, or the sheriff will gather up all the local men and start riding around looking for something that doesn't exist."

"Can't you tell the sheriff they were only thieves?"

"Damn it all, I wish I could, but if I ride into Shelbyville, folks will question why I had such a large sum of money sitting around. It's the same reason I told you we couldn't keep the money in the bank. Folks will figure out what we're up to and beat us to the punch. That's why I need to speak to Brace and the others—to keep things under wraps."

"Boys," Pa said sternly, "don't just stand there gawking. The sun is up, and there's chores that still need to get done while I'm dealing with this nonsense."

Bjorn obeyed, forcing his weak knees to pass through the scene of the crime. Pa had unraveled the truth about the Indians quickly, and it wouldn't take him much longer to unravel the rest of the mystery.

I'm going to get the beating of my life, and everyone around Jackson Lake will hate me.

In the morning light, Bjorn looked around his mother's kitchen, identifying all of the places the money could have been hidden. The ceramic cookie jar above the cast iron stove had been the only one disturbed, and its lid remained on the floor, pointing implicating fingers at him as he walked back to his bedroom.

Bjorn quickly slid on his work trousers, socks, and boots and pulled up his suspenders over his undershirt. By the time he peeked out the window, Pa was already riding hard to the north.

Outside, Gus held the fowling gun as he stood beside mother. Even though he stood in just his undergarments, he'd become a man over the course of the summer, just as big and strong as Pa. At sixteen, he now had hair sprouting on his chest and his arms had doubled in thickness, whereas Bjorn still had thin, stringy arms.

"Put down the gun and go get some clothes on," Ma said as she drew her eyes away from her husband. "You heard your father—he needs you boys to take care of chores. Now go tend to it, and I'll make some breakfast."

"Yes'm," Gustaf said and passed by Bjorn without so much as a glance.

Bjorn walked to the barn alone, his guilt crushing down upon his small shoulders. As with the house, the barn had been upset by the intruders, who left three feed barrels overturned.

Bjorn tended to Goliath first and then the smaller animals, but as he struggled to right one of the overturned barrels, he collapsed and began sobbing.

That was how Gus found him.

"Oh for Pete's sake," Gustaf said with a huff and went right on with the routine.

"Pa's right," Bjorn finally sputtered. "It wasn't Indians who took the money."

"Why do you say that?" Gus asked, pausing in the feedlot.

"I know who took the money."

"What did you do?" Gustaf asked, his face tightening. He charged across the lot, hopped the fence, and grabbed Bjorn by the shirt and suspenders. Gus lifted him up and shook him until they were nose to nose. "What did you do?"

"After church, I went down to McDougal Cave with Brett and Kenny Young, and the Sandford boys were there. We started talking about the railroad, and how—"

"You spilled the beans, didn't you?" Gus asked, his eyes wide with rage, a terrifying sight.

45

"I'm sorry, Gus, I didn't mean to say anything, but when Clancy Brown heard me talking about the depot, he pulled out a knife and held me against a tree."

"Clancy Brown pulled a knife on you?"

Bjorn nodded while sobbing for breath. "They . . . they . . . made me tell them all about the new cottage by the railroad and how *we* was gonna get the train depot instead of Shelbyville."

"And you told them about the money?"

"I told the Young boys, earlier, how we couldn't buy anything on account of putting all of our money in the cookie jar, but when Clancy Brown started pressing me about the new depot, the Young boys told him all about it."

"Do you know what you've done? All sorts of folks have thrown in with Mr. Quiggle, but under the guise of secrecy. Pa was supposed to meet at the cottage tonight with that railroad man and all the other local men. Do you know how fickle these railroad men are? They think they are gods on earth."

"I know, but I didn't think anyone would—"

"Pa and all the others have been holding back money, avoiding the bank so that no one knew what they were going to do. Clancy Brown's father is on the Shelbyville town council."

"I know, but Shelbyville voted against the depot. Why would they rob us if they didn't want the depot?"

"Of course they wanted it."

"But they voted it down."

"Bjorn, the Shelbyville folks were just being penny-pinchers. The railroad guys were trying to force ten thousand dollars out of them to secure the depot, but the folks in Shelbyville called their bluff by not giving them the money. They believed they'd still have to build the depot anyway. Clancy Brown, the Sandford Boys, and your Young buddies—their folks all own businesses in Shelbyville. And you went and spilled the beans."

"I didn't understand."

"You've messed things up, Bjorn. Now hurry up and finish chores so we can go fix this. And don't say a word to Ma."

While Bjorn finished taking care of the animals, Gustaf saddled up Goliath, but not for field work. Shame kept Bjorn from asking any other questions, and in a few minutes, he meekly followed Gus back to the house.

The beauty of Jackson Lake mocked their predicament as the sun rose in the eastern sky, reflecting off the placid waters. The grove of young oaks planted between the homestead and the shore had thickened just over the course of the summer, replacing the patch of mighty cottonwoods they'd felled for lumber. Ducks and geese dodged in and out of the reeds, and a bass jumped from a weed patch, unaware of the drama affecting their human neighbors.

"Don't worry about the money, boys," Ma said after they sat down and glumly stared at their plates. In the time they'd done chores, Ma had tidied the kitchen, placing the cookie jar lid above the stove where the big jar should have been. Ma had also dressed during the time, wearing her long-sleeve cotton shirt and skirt with a brown smock that took the brunt of cooking and gardening duties during a typical workday. Her black hair, with a few strands of gray, had been tightly pulled behind her head in a bun, leaving a part down the middle. When she had her hair down at night, she looked a decade younger. Now she again looked like Ma.

Ma had been born Erin Kirkpatrick to a Scottish family in nearby Mapleton, and her breakfast reflected her heritage. Bjorn ate the link sausage first, then shoveled in her baked beans before turning to the bowl of porridge she offered directly from the stove. "We almost lost everything a few years ago when the grasshoppers came, and after that, there were wildfires. We've tucked away plenty of money in the bank, and God permitting, we'll have our best harvest yet, not to mention how well the livestock has been doing. Eat up, I'm sure your father will get to the bottom of all of this craziness."

Just as Bjorn finished with the porridge, she placed a plate of tattie scones on the table, which both boys snatched into their hands, stuffing them into their pockets for a midmorning snack.

Gus formed a plan. "Pa wanted us to go down to the lake and cut some more cottonwoods. I'm going to saddle up Goliath for the hauling. Keep the rifle handy in case those thieves come back. Just fire off a shot and we'll come running. We'll bring the fowling gun with us."

Scones in pocket, Gus rose and walked toward the door. Bjorn did the same and had to run to keep up with him as they headed toward the barn. Once there, Gustaf picked up a double-headed ax and handed it to him.

"Get this head off the ax while I saddle up Goliath."

Removing a metal ax-head took a considerable amount of effort and focus from Bjorn. To reverse it, Bjorn had to pry the metal out, a bit at a time, with a flat screwdriver. He'd managed to withdraw a half-inch of metal when Gus stood over him.

"Let me do it," Gustaf said, snatching the ax away. In just a few seconds, his strong hands managed to pry the metal insert apart, and then he turned the ax-head against a stall railing and popped the handle off, tossing the blade onto the floor. "Let's go."

Before Bjorn even understood what was happening, Goliath's heavy but slow gallop took them on a direct path toward the Blue Earth River.

Two against the Shelbyville gang? We'll get the tar beaten out of us.

Straight west of Jackson Lake, the Blue Earth River crossed a shallow bed of gravel known as Dodd's Fjord.

"Are you looking for tracks like Pa?" Bjorn asked as Goliath descended the steep slope of the river and into the shallow water of Dodd's Fjord.

"I know what I'm looking for," Gus said sharply, which shut Bjorn's mouth.

He's going right to McDougal Cave.

In the novel *Huckleberry Finn*, Injun Joe's hideout was a large cave complex along the Mississippi River where the fiend hid his loot. The local Shelbyville boys, having read the Twain novel, named their smaller version after the tale. Bjorn had been to the sandstone cave twice, most recently when he was accosted by Clancy Brown, the obnoxious town bully.

The Shelbyville boys loved the location because of the privacy. The woods were especially thick around McDougal Cave, and even from the ridge overlooking the river, the entrance of the cave could not be seen. Outside the cave, there was a natural rocky step, where the boys could all sit or use it as a platform from which to jump into the river.

Before reaching the bend downstream from the cave, Gus stopped the horse and hopped off into the knee-deep water. He reached into the saddlebag and withdrew the fowling gun, handing it to Bjorn.

"I'm going to fix this, but I need you to do exactly what I tell you, understand?"

Bjorn nodded, his hands shaking with fear.

"I want you to stay here and count to two hundred, and then I want you to have Goliath walk slowly upstream to the cave."

"Where are you going to be?"

Gus quickly explained his plan, which did not bring any comfort to Bjorn, especially when his brother pulled the ax handle from the leather straps of the saddlebag.

Bjorn did as commanded and closed his eyes while he counted to two hundred, not to avoid seeing anything but just to calm his nerves. When he closed his eyes, he could picture Clancy Brown's yellow teeth and the cold blade that had been pressed to his throat.

One ninety-eight, one ninety-nine, two hundred. Bjorn opened his eyes and, with his heels, nudged Goliath forward through the current.

As he came around the bend, he saw McDougal Cave, and with it, his worst fears were confirmed. Brett and Kenny Young sat with all five Sandford boys, who ranged from ages seven to seventeen. Several alcohol bottles and stolen loot from area farms were strewn about near the cave. Up in the trees, several horses were tied. The biggest boy amongst them was Clancy Brown, who sat up, bare chested, from his spot along the rocky step.

"Look what the cat dragged in," Clancy called out. "Whatcha doing, Forsberg? Hunting for Indians?"

Kenny Young still had war paint on his face, and a few of the Sandford boys had feathers in their hair, which they quickly pulled out upon seeing the intruder coming up the river with a gun in his hands.

"I know it was you, Clancy. I know you snuck in and stole it."

"Stole what?" Clancy said, standing up in defiance.

"I want the cookie jar back."

"Cookies!" Clancy shouted, causing the other boys to laugh. "Why don't you come on up here and take a look? Ain't no cookies here."

Bjorn did as ordered and guided Goliath to the western shore, opposite of McDougal Cave, where he hopped off Goliath and tied him to the thin branches of a bush. Still holding the fowling gun, Bjorn began to wade into the water.

"You think you're going to scare us with that old buckshot gun?" Clancy asked.

"No," Bjorn answered. "But Gus said I should use it to keep you all distracted."

With the stealth of a panther, Gus leapt down from the ridge above the rocky step, pushing Brett Young off his feet and into the Blue Earth River below. Before Clancy could even turn, Gus swung sideways, catching him in the side near his right kidney.

The rest of the Shelbyville boys looked on in awe as Gus wailed away on their leader like an enraged jungle ape. A dozen blows were landed by the time Brett Young came out of the water to stare down the barrel of Bjorn's shaking fowling gun.

Back on the rocky step, Gus turned the ax handle on Allen Sandford, the eldest brother. The first blow struck his defensive arms, the second glanced off his ear and struck his collarbone, but the third was caught by Henry Sandford, who grabbed the handle before Gus could swing again.

Gus let go, elbowing Henry in the face, turning his nose into a geyser of blood and sending the three youngest brothers running for town. Even without his ax handle, Gus still knocked out Allen Sandford's teeth, leaving him crumpled on ledge beside his gang leader.

Henry feebly swung the ax handle back at Gus, who caught it in his hand and jerked it away from the younger boy, causing him to almost fall from the ledge.

"Clancy made me do it, Bjorn," Brett Young said, terror in his eyes at seeing his protection transform into two bloody piles. "We weren't going to keep any of it. We were going to blame it on Indians and say we found the loot. Clancy said . . ."

Brett stopped talking when he saw Gus, flecked with blood, striding through the water toward him. Whimpering, he ducked low and held his hands up in submission. Gus had grown up working the land each day of his life, while the Shelbyville boys grew up running around town, terrorizing others.

In one hand, Gus held the ax handle, but in the other, he held the cookie jar.

Brett Young did not take the beating he deserved but only cowered as Gus walked by him. Bjorn accepted the cookie jar, and his brother climbed up on the horse.

It wasn't until they got home that they discovered the jar held more money than the Forsberg family had put in it. Pa, who kept his hands on his hips during the whole explanation, shook his head as he said, "I don't know if I feel shame or pride right now. Bjorn, you're going to come with me and look our neighbors in the eyes like a man and explain to them what happened."

Shortly after supper, Sigmund and Bjorn Forsberg arrived at George Quiggle's property, where a new cottage had been built just off the railroad tracks. Outside of the small cottage, a dozen local farmers had already gathered to watch as father and son rode up.

Mr. Quiggle walked up to Pa to steady the horse, "Heard you Jackson Lake folks had some trouble last night."

"Bjorn is here to set things right. Go ahead, Bjorn."

So Bjorn told his neighbors—William Busse, Hiram Bornt, J.C. Nobles, Chester Bailey, Edward Brace, Laomi and Loren Smith, and John Durr—how he had spilled the beans to the Shelbyville boys and how his heroic brother Gus had gone into the den of thieves to retrieve the money.

It was agreed that despite Bjorn's foolishness, he and Gus had rightly saved the day.

The Shelbyville boys had robbed three houses along Jackson Lake that night, including the home of Hiram Bornt. Although Hiram learned the truth directly from Pa earlier that morning, he still came to the meeting with empty pockets but with collateral—a red cow with broken horns.

"I'm sorry, Mr. Bornt," Bjorn said as he returned the mystery money to its owner.

"All's well that ends well," Mr. Bornt said, patting Bjorn on the shoulder.

Pa's hundred dollars was given to men who'd loaned him money to survive the hardships inflicted by the grasshopper swarms in previous summers. Those men then placed their money on the table and signed their names to the secret document.

"Will it be enough?" One of the men asked during the process.

"It won't be enough," another stated as George Quiggle focused on recording each donation.

"The railroad wanted ten thousand dollars from the folks in Shelbyville. This isn't nearly enough."

"It isn't what was expected," George Quiggle said when he finished counting, "but a bird in the hand is worth two in the bush."

Just before dusk, a man from the St. Paul and Sioux City Railroad arrived wearing a fancy suit and polished shoes. "So this house will be given to my station agent?" He asked inspecting the workmanship. Many of the beams and boards had come from trees Bjorn and Gus felled earlier in the summer.

"This cottage, forty acres of land, a contract, and our gratitude," George Quiggle answered proudly.

"Then, gentlemen, you'll have your depot," the man from the railroad declared, sealing the deal. "What will you call your new town?"

"Jackson Lake," a voice answered.

Another offered, "Jacksonville."

Mr. Richardson, who owned the local mercantile store, stood up and cleared his throat. "Gentlemen, we've all taken a risk by negotiating the depot rights to be built here, instead of Shelbyville, but I've put my business and reputation on the line. If I'm going to risk moving my business to a town that doesn't exist, I'd like a say in its name."

"Your suggestion?" asked George Quiggle.

"I was born in Amboy, Illinois. I say we name the new town Amboy."

Although twenty-five local residents signed their name to the document, Robert Richardson became the first business owner in the new town when it was agreed to name the new depot Amboy.

Bjorn knew he deserved the beating given to Clancy Brown, but instead, Pa put a hand on his shoulder, squeezing gently in an unexpected show of pride. Like Richardson, Pa's name wasn't on the contract, but he'd also helped birth a new town into existence and steal the future away from the rogues in Shelbyville.

With the secret contract finalized, everyone stepped outside of the railway cottage, which according to the contract, would be occupied within the month. Bjorn looked around George Quiggle's vacant plot of land, trying to imagine a future with a train depot, grain elevator, and Richardson's mercantile store. The twelve vacant city blocks he'd seen written upon paper would be filled with colorful houses and vital businesses, right beside the new rail line that stretched between Mankato and Blue Earth City.

The mood was jovial as the twenty-five signers and their retinue lingered around the lit cottage and under the summer stars. When the railroad agent finally found an opportunity to leave, William Busse called out loudly, "Sir! You forgot your red cow!"

The railroad agent, with a wad of money and contract, only scoffed, "What am I supposed to do with a cow with broken horns? Keep it, folks, it is now Amboy city property."

Everyone chuckled, especially the previous owner, Hiram Bornt, who'd given up his cow in desperation, only to have his stolen money returned to his pocketbook.

"Hiram," George Quiggle called out, "would you like your red cow back?"

"You heard the man—it's property of the city of Amboy now. Besides, it's an old cow and only worth its weight in hamburger."

"Hamburger?" Pa said, turning to the other folks gathered around. "The night is still young, and we have some celebrating to do. Enough secrecy. Let's gather up our families, light a bonfire that can be seen in Shelbyville, and celebrate until dawn."

THE RED COW BURGER

Recipe courtesy of Lisa Lindberg, owner, The Amboy Cottage Café, Amboy, Minnesota

Directions

Thoughtfully select locally grown grass-fed beef (90% lean).

Shape raw meat into 6- to 8-ounce patties, ¾-inch thick.

Depress centers to ½ inch.

Grill in a cast iron pan for several minutes until browned.

Sprinkle with freshly ground pepper and garlic salt, turn, and cook to medium when juices run clear.

Turning and pressing lightly several times will speed up cooking.

Place on toasted homemade bread slices and top with cheese.

Add grilled onion, mushrooms, or pepper slices.

Sauerkraut, blue cheese, olives, bacon, lettuce, tomato, and pickles can top the red cow too!

Date Night

SEED OF DOUBT

By Cheryl Ullyot

HE BROKE UP with her over dinner at her favorite restaurant, Barraco, a charming rustic bistro located on one of Montreal's oldest romantic streets.

"We need to talk," he said, while they shared the organic artisanal charcuterie platter.

"It's not you; it's me," he said, as she stared blankly at her red cabbage, watercress, goat cheese, and smoked nut salad.

By the time he finished his spiel, tears were trickling down her cheeks into her Pappardelle Vesuvio.

Ross Simmons was a flight attendant's dream. A co-pilot on the Boeing 757, he was tall, athletic with thick dark hair and brown eyes. Walking through the airport in his navy-blue pilot's uniform he looked straight out of central casting. Perpetually tanned, he looked as though he could have just stepped off a beach in Puerto Vallarta, which wasn't far from the truth, since Mexico was his favorite layover spot. He flew his dates to exotic places for the weekend in his private plane.

He was funny, self-deprecating, and popular with the pilots and flight attendants alike. Deep down, Ashley knew that he was a womanizer, vain, self-centered, and narcissistic. His reputation around the airline was of sleeping with one flight attendant after another, occasionally keeping two of them wrapped around his finger. Yet he never seemed to suffer any consequences. The other pilots envied his prowess, and the women all thought they'd be the one to change him. And like the others before her, Ashley fell for his charms. She was sure this time was different. Hadn't he said that she was special?

They walked the few blocks back to their layover hotel, making mundane conversation. He acted as though everything was fine. Just co-workers out for a bite to eat. When they got up to their floor, he stopped at his room and dug out the key.

"Can't we discuss this more?" she asked, as he opened his hotel room door. He blocked her way. "I don't understand, why so sudden? Did I do something?"

"Like I said, I just need some space. Look, I'm really tired and I have to get up at 6:00 a.m."

"That never bothered you before."

"Look," he said, turning cold, "we've had a nice time tonight, and I just bought you an expensive meal. Let's be mature about this and end this like adults."

"I can't believe you're doing this to me," she said, her voice sounding shrill.

"Shhhh! Don't go all hysterical on me. You don't want to get us both fired." His eyes darted up and down the hotel corridor to see if anyone was within earshot. "Now, grow up. We've had a good time, but like I said, I need some time to myself." He backed into his room and slammed the door, leaving her standing in the hallway stunned.

• • • • •

In the morning, he flew off to New York while she worked a flight back to Minneapolis.

Back home she called her friend Freddie to vent.

"Honey, I warned you. Ross is the biggest cheat there is. He doesn't want his alone time. He's been seeing Caroline Avery. He's taking her to Cabo in a couple of weeks."

Caroline Avery. Only her best friend from flight attendant training. How dare he take her friend on a romantic holiday that was planned for them. How dare he humiliate her this way. No wonder he was in such a hurry to dump her.

Ashley picked up the Orrefors crystal decanter that she had brought back from a layover in Sweden and threw it against the wall. Then she went into the bathroom and vomited.

As the days went on, she vacillated between wanting him back and wanting revenge.

One night she drank too much and called him, but he didn't answer. Even after leaving several messages, he never returned her calls.

She found a pair of his sunglasses stuck between her couch cushions and put them in her purse. Then one evening, coming home from the grocery store, she found herself driving by his townhouse. The lights were on. She sat out front thinking. If she could just see him one more time. She could use those shades as an excuse. She got out of her car and walked up to the front door. Just as she was about to ring the doorbell, she saw movement through the window. He was walking into the living room carrying a glass of red wine. Perfect. Then another figure entered the room. It was Caroline Avery, laughing and carrying the bottle of wine in her hand. Ashley froze as they stood by the fireplace.

Kissing.

She brought the sunglasses home and stomped on them.

· · · · ·

One day as she was reorganizing her flight bag, she found a package of apricot pits that she had bought with Ross at a health food store in Canada.

"You should get those. They're supposedly the new superfood," he had said.

"Looks like almonds. But sixteen dollars? Kind of an expensive snack," Ashley mused.

"You know, the Hunza people from the Himalayan region in northern Pakistan are known for longevity and good health and value these seeds greatly. Have you ever had *dokka*? A traditional Egyptian snack? They mix coriander seeds with salt and apricot kernels."

Ross was a health nut and a real know-it-all when it came to vitamins and health food. And to think that used to impress her.

"Well, I guess I'll get them then," she said, taking his advice as gospel.

"They're better for you than those cheese curls you're so fond of."

Now weeks later, she was about to throw out the unopened package, when she noticed a warning on the back.

"DO NOT CONSUME MORE THAN TWO TO THREE KERNELS A DAY!" it read. "EATING TOO MANY APRICOT KERNELS MAY CAUSE ACUTE CYANIDE POISONING."

What? She couldn't believe it. She was pretty sure that Ross wasn't aware of the dangers. Now curious, she decided to Google it and found alarming reports: A man in Australia ended up in the hospital after eating too many seeds and had to be treated for cyanide poisoning. In fact, Australia banned them in 2015. She read on. Apricot kernels naturally contain a compound called amygdalin, which has the potential to release cyanide when ingested by humans. Small amounts are detoxified by the human body, but high doses can be lethal. Some of the side effects listed were headache, dizziness, nausea, weakness, mental confusion, convulsions, and an inability to breathe.

Her first thought was to warn Ross. Admittedly, it was another excuse to go over and see him.

Maybe he'd had a change of heart. Surely, he missed her by now. She tossed the bag of apricot seeds in the trash.

Her phone rang. It was Freddie.

"Hi, sweetie. Did you know we're flying together on Wednesday?"

"Yes, the La Guardia turnaround? I love that trip. Leave at 9:00 a.m., home by 5:00 p.m."

"Well, you might not love it so much this time. Are you sitting down?"

"Why?" she asked.

"I checked the crew orders. Coming back from New York we get a different cockpit. Guess who the co-pilot is?"

"Ross?"

"You got it. What a jerk. I heard he and Caroline are running a marathon in Maui next month."

Ashley's muscles tightened. She thought back to when she tried to please Ross by taking up running.

He had chided her for only being able to run a mile before getting winded.

After she hung up, Ashley grabbed a bag of cheese curls and popped a few in her mouth.

"Screw you, Ross," she muttered, as she dug the apricot pits out of the garbage and put them back in her flight bag.

· · · · ·

Wednesday

Ashley pulled the first-class curtain closed, removed the bag of apricot seeds from her flight bag, and placed it on the galley counter. The meal trays for the cockpit sat on the galley table. She unwrapped the salads and desserts on each tray while she waited for the casseroles to heat.

Suddenly, the curtain was yanked open and a large, grinning, red face appeared.

"Hey, honey. What are you doing hiding in here? How about another round before lunch?"

Mr. Coburn, the first-class passenger in 2B, thrust his empty glass in her face.

"Double scotch on the rocks."

Startled, she grabbed his glass and began to replenish it with ice and scotch. The basket of peanuts and pretzels sat on the counter.

"Oh, and I'll take a couple more of these. There are only about four peanuts in each bag these days and who likes pretzels? Whatever happened to the almonds?"

"Sorry, that's what they give me to serve. But I'll be bringing lunch shortly."

"So, what's on the menu? Prime rib?" he said, laughing.

"A turkey sandwich and potato salad."

He scrunched up his nose as if he had smelled a skunk.

"Hey, who gets those?" he said, edging his way into the galley to check out the pilot trays.

"Those are the pilot meals. They have a long day of flying, and they need to eat too."

He noticed the stickers on the trays: *Captain—steak. Co-pilot—vegetarian lasagna.*

"So why does only the captain get the steak?"

"The pilots get different meals in case one of them gets food poisoning." Ashley was getting impatient.

"Well, la-di-da, they get steak and lasagna, and we get a lousy turkey sandwich. "

She handed him his drink, and he was about to take his seat when he noticed the bag of apricot seeds on the counter next to the snack basket.

"Hey, here's the almonds. Looks like you've been holding out on me," he said, picking up the bag.

Ashley reached over and snatched it out of his hands.

"Sorry, these are mine, I brought them from home. You'd better take your seat now, sir. We might be experiencing some turbulence soon."

Glutton, she thought.

After he left, she pulled the curtain closed again. Then she counted out eight apricot seeds and sprinkled them on the co-pilot's salad.

The cockpit door opened and out stepped Captain Andrews.

Ashley had flown with the older man several times and had such admiration for him. He was a fatherly figure who always treated his crew with respect. Lovingly spoke with pride about his wife of forty years and his four kids. He was everything that Ross wasn't.

"Hi there, Ashley," he said, peeking in the galley. "I just stepped out for a minute to use the lav. How's everything going? Can I do anything for you?"

"No, sir. I'm just heating your crew meals. Would you like me to bring them up?"

"Just leave them on the counter. I'll take them up when I go back to the cockpit. "

"Will do." Ashley put the casseroles on the trays and smiled. Then she went about her duties, serving first class.

She looked at her watch. Not much longer before landing. She wondered how Ross was feeling after his lunch. She didn't want to kill him. Just make him sick and ruin his upcoming trip to Cabo.

He'd probably start to feel the effects of the pits after they landed.

The passengers finished their meals and were sleeping or reading, except of course, for Mr. Coburn, who continued to demand more drinks and more snacks.

Ashley went into the lavatory to freshen up her makeup and comb her hair. Her thoughts turned to Ross. Serves him right, she thought. He brought this on himself. Cheater! When he gets home, he'll probably just think he has the flu or food poisoning from the lasagna. Macho man may not even go to the doctor.

They were starting their descent into Minneapolis when she heard the ding that signaled the cockpit was calling. She'd let Freddie answer it. She was busy fixing Mr. Coburn one last scotch. I wonder if he'll be able to walk off the plane, she thought.

Freddie came rushing up the aisle. He ducked into the galley and closed the curtain behind him.

"That was the cockpit. Something is wrong. Sounds serious. They didn't say what, but they are getting clearance to land now. The EMTs are meeting the plane, so keep the passengers seated until they come on and things get settled.

"No other details?" she asked, her heart pounding.

"No, just make the announcement for everyone to prepare for landing and take your seat."

He hurried down the aisle with a garbage bag picking up dirty glasses and checking seat belts.

The plane landed and they taxied to a gate. Ashley told the passengers to remain seated.

The agent opened the front cabin door, and the EMTs were waiting outside with a gurney.

"Excuse us, please, coming through. Keep the passengers back," they said, as the cockpit door was flung open from inside.

Ashley stood back waiting. After a bit of jockeying around and commotion, she saw them wheeling out the gurney.

She made an announcement for the passengers to stay in their seats. She could see the heads craning to see what was happening as she looked down the aisle. Standing by the cockpit door, she felt someone's hand on her shoulder. She turned to see Ross, looking shaken. Her mouth flew open as she ran off the plane to see Captain Andrews being wheeled up the jetway.

She scurried back.

"What happened to him?" she asked Ross.

"I don't know. I think he had a heart attack. He said he felt dizzy and nauseous. Or maybe it was the lasagna. Who knows? "

"The lasagna? But . . . he had a steak," she said, now feeling dizzy herself.

"Actually, we traded meal trays. I told him I was on the Keto diet now and he's such a nice guy he swapped with me."

Oh my God, thought Ashley. I hope I haven't killed him.

"I'll make an announcement and let the passengers know it's okay to deplane now," Ross said.

As the passengers flooded the aisle, Ashley heard a call button ringing. Coming from row 2. The passenger in seat 2A was frantic.

"Flight attendant, you need to do something! I think this man is dead."

Ashley looked down at Mr. Coburn, who was at best, unconscious.

"What happened here?" she asked.

"I don't know. He kept sneaking into the galley grabbing almonds while you were in the restroom."

She looked down and saw a handful of apricot pits in his fist.

CLASSIC LASAGNA

Recipe courtesy of Chef Tim McHugh and Drs. Basir and Mohiba Tareen, owners of Amore Uptown, Minneapolis, Minnesota

Ingredients

6 cups spicy Bolognese sauce

4 cups shredded mozzarella cheese

2 cups whole milk ricotta cheese

2 cups grated Parmesan cheese

1 large egg

½ cup minced Italian flat-leaf parsley

12 lasagna noodle sheets

Directions

Preheat oven to 350 degrees F.

Make the cheese mixture. In a large bowl, add 1 cup mozzarella, the ricotta, ¼ cup Parmesan, 2 tablespoons of parsley, and the egg. Stir until well mixed.

Cook the pasta sheets al dente, according to package directions.

Assemble the lasagna. In a 13 x 9 inch baking dish, add a very thin layer of Bolognese (about ¼ cup). Layer 4 lasagna noodles, ⅓ of ricotta mixture, and 1½ cups of Bolognese. Repeat layering twice.

Add a final layer of remaining noodle sheets, Bolognese, 1 cup mozzarella, and ¼ cup Parmesan.

Cover with foil that has been sprayed with nonstick cooking spray. Bake for 45 minutes. Remove the foil. Add remaining cheese and minced parsley, bake 15 more minutes uncovered.

Let the lasagna cool for 15–20 minutes before cutting.

AMORE SPICY BOLOGNESE SAUCE

Ingredients

2 tablespoons olive oil

5 tablespoons butter

1 cup chopped onion

1⅓ cup chopped celery

1⅓ cup chopped carrot

1½ pounds lean ground beef

1 tablespoon salt

2 tablespoons ground black pepper

2 tablespoons ground nutmeg

2 cups whole milk

2 cups dry white wine

3 cups Italian plum tomatoes, cut up, with juice

Directions

In a large soup pot, combine oil, butter, and chopped onion over medium heat. Stir until onion has become translucent. Add chopped celery and carrot. Cook for about 4 minutes, stirring all the vegetables to coat them well.

Add ground beef, salt, and pepper. Crumble meat with a wood spoon, stir well until beef has lost its red color.

Add milk and let mixture simmer gently, stirring frequently. When the milk has completely bubbled away, add the nutmeg and stir.

Add white wine and let simmer until wine has evaporated. Add Italian plum tomatoes and stir thoroughly to coat all ingredients. When tomatoes begin to bubble, turn heat down to lowest of simmers. Cook uncovered for 3 hours, stirring occasionally. Check seasonings before serving.

LUNCH WITH ROMAN LEW

By Jeanne Shields

INSPECTOR SADIE OSBORNE opened the mini fridge near her desk and stared at her lunch. Lew, her partner, rolled his chair over. It was two in the afternoon, and they were just now finding time to eat.

"You had that yesterday," he said.

"A salad, yes."

He relaxed into the webbed office chair, his fingers tapping on the arm. "Yup."

"We are what we eat."

His eyes fell to his black Rockport shoes as they gave a good push away from the fridge. "I'm hungry. If I don't eat, I'll be useless for the rest of the day."

She noticed the shelf where he always placed his lunch was empty. "You didn't bring a lunch."

"It's on my kitchen counter." He stood, his medium-sized frame shadowing her. "Let's go out."

"I brought lunch."

"Add cottage cheese and a pineapple ring, and I'll mistake you for my grandma." He pulled her chair out from her desk.

"My salad is fine, but thank you for the offer."

He opened the office door for her and waited. Finally, he said. "We need some space from our cases. I'll buy."

She narrowed her eyes. Lew wasn't the easiest person to read or trust. He was unconventional. "Earlier today, you said something about liking oysters. I don't like oysters."

"I like all living creatures. That doesn't mean I want to eat them. I like you, for instance."

"Am I going to regret this?"

"It's a lunch."

When Sadie began working with Lew, she noticed people gave him sideways glances, as she was doing now. They walked down to the parking garage, and Lew pulled out the keys to his dark blue RAV4. They headed to Third Avenue and continued north across the Third Avenue Bridge as it became Central Avenue. They made a beeline to Lowry and parked in the lot of a big church. He led her around to the storefronts, and they stopped at a door with a red awning and gold lettering spelling Sen Yai Sen Lek. Inspector Lew had a craving for Thai.

He smiled. "Do you trust me now?"

"I'll definitely trust you when my lunch goes on your credit card."

"And so it will."

Lew held the door as Sadie entered the restaurant. He waved at a man in a baseball cap, and the man waved back. She watched another man come in for a late lunch, collect his takeout, and leave. Someone snuck through a doorway that Lew told her led to Dipped and Debris sandwich shop.

They sat at a table for four. A man in a baseball cap stopped by the table and placed a menu in front of her. "Nice to see you, Lew."

"Likewise." Lew glanced at Sadie. "Osborne, meet Joe. Joe, Osborne."

The man nodded politely at Sadie and then asked, "How's Pops?"

"Out of the hospital."

"Good. Stop at the sandwich shop, I'll have a Dipped waiting. I know how he likes his Chicago-style Italian beef."

"Thanks, Joe. I'll run it up to him."

Joe smiled, and then followed a call from the staff.

Sadie didn't know Pops was in the hospital. She didn't even know who Pops was. She and Lew had worked together two months, and she still knew virtually nothing about him.

Lew pointed at her menu. "Khao Soi is good. Pad Thai, of course."

"Who's Pops?" She tried to look into his movie star blue eyes, but they remained on the menu. She stared instead at the scar near the intersection of his forehead and his untamed thick black hair. When she'd asked him how he got the scar, he told her a pot landed on him. That was it. Just like now. No real facts, just fragments.

"My grandfather." He answered her. That was a start. "What are you having?"

"What's wrong with him?"

"Cancer. Maybe I'll order two meals."

"What kind of cancer?"

He looked up at her. "Prostate. They got it. He'll be fine. I'll tell him you're thinking about him."

Again, she was suspicious. "Two meals. How late are we working tonight?"

"Not to worry."

What did "not to worry" mean? She ignored the menu, instead watched the foot traffic outside. When she was first assigned to Northeast Minneapolis as a patrol officer, her partner gave her a tour of the area. And every night they worked together he added a little more to the tour. His name was Paul Dudek. He told her where the battles were fought between high schools, where to buy the finest meat in the city, which bar promised the most fun, and which church had the best fish fry, flat out. He showed her the lover's lane where he and his wife, then girlfriend, conceived their first child. He called the community Nordeast and told her it had gone from an old eastern European immigrant stronghold, to what it was now, an artist and mixed immigrant community. He was an old timer, he told her. He'd look around the neighborhoods where he grew up and talked about how he missed the Sunday masses and the rosary society donuts. As he showed her the streets, she looked around and wondered how many generations of immigrants, from how many countries, had started their lives on these same streets.

Lew tapped on the table to get her attention. "Have you decided?"

Sadie smiled. "I think I'm going to trust you."

"That's a start."

She took a quick glance from the menu to Lew, and then back down again. Did her lack of trust in him originate at the station where he was considered a psycho, or was she projecting her mother's fear of the misfit? Maybe it was her fear of being the misfit herself. Maybe she was putting too much burden on Lew. He was just a co-worker.

Never mind. It didn't matter. It was a job, one she liked.

Her mother had recoiled when Sadie finally broke the news that she wanted to become an investigator. This wasn't what she'd planned for her youngest child. "Wouldn't your father be proud to see you as a lawyer and then maybe a judge? You're the brightest. A common cop and now inspector?" How was her mother going to explain to their friends, the sight of little blonde, beautiful Sarah, the homecoming queen, on the news wearing a baseball cap and a sidearm?

Sadie's father, an attorney, couldn't quite warm up to her new title either. It wasn't because he worried for her personal safety or well-being. Her father's advice was, "Let somebody else do the grunt work. Be a prosecutor if you want to do the whole justice thing. Do it for a few years and move on."

Lew was staring at his phone. He wasn't that much older than Sadie's twenty-seven years, but he was already making a name for himself. His solve and convict rate was the best in the department. She worked hard with him, and they seemed to be a good team, but he was a lot quicker than she was. He saw things that would never cross her mind. Most days, she felt lucky to be assigned with him.

He told her when they were first assigned together that she should call him Lew. Not Roman? she asked. Not Roman. Never Roman. She told him he could call her Sadie. She had yet to hear him call her that. Generally, it was Inspector Osborne. At first, when he said it at the station, people turned. They looked at her and looked at him, like it was impossible to fathom her as an investigator or maybe the two of them working together. Soon enough, though, when he used her name with the title, they didn't get a glance.

This particular day, Sadie and Lew had been assembling a case that had begun six months earlier against a man who'd gotten into an altercation with his neighbor. He had whacked the neighbor with an ax he was using to chop wood. Sadie had been the responding officer at the time and had taken control of the scene. What she didn't know then, before becoming an inspector, was how to think in terms of a case 24/7. One fact had to fit into another, like a jigsaw puzzle. Lew had been the investigator assigned to the case. She remembered him asking her questions and waiting a little too patiently for the answers, like she was a simpleton.

"Where's the weapon?"

She looked around. She'd been busy trying to keep the suspect on the ground until another officer arrived and then had been working on the victim until medical arrived. "I'm not sure."

He nodded. "It's okay. I see you've been busy."

"I'll looked around."

"No. No. You talk to the wife. I'll carry on here."

"Good, yes, I'll do that." She pulled out her notebook and walked toward a car that had just pulled into the driveway. It suddenly occurred to her that the woman didn't know what was going on, that her husband was on the way to the hospital and was probably already deceased. Sadie was going to be giving this poor woman the news. She glanced back at Lew. He appeared engrossed in the ax. As she walked toward the woman, she felt his movie star blue eyes on her back. He was watching what she did and how she did it. She'd show that SOB what kind of cop she was.

Sadie guessed she did show him. And now they were assigned together.

Lew broke into her thoughts. "You seem preoccupied."

"No."

He nodded, his eyes narrowing ever so slightly. "So, what are you getting?"

"I'm going to start off with the Burning Brothers Pyro."

He smiled. "That'll take the edge off."

She returned the smile and looked down at the menu. "Actually, I'll have the Khao Soi and sparkling water."

"Good choice."

The server, a young woman with wild punk- hair of every impossible color, stopped at the table. She and Lew had a friendly conversation. She told him about classes she was taking at the university, and he asked about her stuck-up ex-boyfriend. They laughed.

Sadie pointed at the menu. "I think I'll have Khao Soi with fried tofu. And water is good."

"And how about you, Roman?"

Roman? Roman?

Lew smiled his perfect smile at the server. "I'll have Pad Gratiem Prik Thai. I'll take it with chicken."

"You liked the suggestion I offered you the last time you were here."

"I did." His perfect smile got bigger, and Sadie instantly got a clearer idea of what Roman Lew really craved. She half listened to them chat while she read a text from her best friend, Ashley, who was getting married in August. It was May, and they were doing a dress fitting for the fourth time. This time all four bridesmaids would be in one place at the same time. Giggles. Planning a sleep over. Yippee. She texted a "great" back to her friend.

She caught Lew watching her. "Sorry. A friend. I'm her maid of honor. Just some arrangements."

"Well, that will be fun."

She shrugged then smiled.

"Won't it?"

"Well. Honestly? Where I come from everybody has an important title or is married to someone with an important title. I don't, and I'm not married to anyone who does, so I don't fit anymore. Everybody knows it, and I know it. So, will it be fun?"

"Maybe if you get extra drunk. Bring some Pyro with you, enough for everyone."

She laughed. "My mother warned me this would happen, and I didn't listen. I think this wedding is making it crystal clear."

"Do you regret the life your chose?"

"No. It's just hard to be out in the cold."

In the short time she'd worked with Lew, she had found herself revealing more to him than she thought she should about her personal life. She always wondered if she would regret it. What did she know about him? He graduated from college with a double major in criminal science and philosophy, spent time in the Navy, came home, and then became a cop. He told her all this one night, while they sat in the car waiting for the wife of a suspect to put out the garbage. There was no time to ask questions. When the wife went back inside the house, they quickly grabbed the garbage, like thieves in the night, and the moment was over. She did the math, though. He was thirty-two.

"Let's sit here." A chair hit her chair as a man sat down. No apologies. She looked at Lew. He smiled.

"Where's the waitress?" asked a husky voice. She didn't turn around but guessed he was a big man by the force against her chair and the feel of him when he leaned back and then forward to move the chair. She could smell his sweat. He shifted in his chair, knocking hers again. She moved her chair forward. It was in between lunch and dinner. There were at least twelve empty tables, and he chose to sit next to them.

"We could just go to a fast food place." This voice was higher, with a nasal tone.

"You think they're going to have anything like this in the fields?"

"Not sure what they got there. Never been there." And then the higher voice added in a contrite way, as if he'd gotten a look from the other man. "I'm fine staying here."

Lew's phone danced on the table. He picked it up without a word and read the text. It wasn't a call from the station, or her phone would have gone off at the same time.

Her fingers tapped lightly on the table. "Where's our food I wonder?"

He was half listening. "It should be up any second."

The server went to the table with the men. They ordered to go. Lew looked up. His eyes shifted to follow the young woman as she walked back toward the kitchen. This time no smile.

Lew suddenly chuckled loudly. It was as she imagined a drunk Roman Lew would laugh. "I just got a meme. Wait until you see this."

He slid his phone Sadie's way, and she read the text. *Saw your car in the lot behind. The big guy who just walked in is wanted for robbery,*

attempted murder. We don't know if he's packing. Stay in place. That's an
order. We're moving people out from the back.

She made a face at Lew and pointed silently behind her. He nodded.
"Funny right?"

"Oh, cute," she said, dragging the word cute out.

Another text came in. She read it and handed the phone back to
Lew.

His name is Stanley Kowal. His mother still lives in the area, and he
stopped to see her, in and out, no time to say hello, or good-bye, took a duffle
bag and left.

Sadie's hand instantly moved up to her chest. She knew she was
wearing her vest because she wore it out of habit, but she checked
anyway. The two remaining diners left through the front door, and she
thanked the god of every religion that it was late in the afternoon and
the place was now empty.

It had become quiet. No sounds of pots. No laugh at a joke. She
wondered about the sandwich shop when she heard its door open.
After a long pause, the door closed.

Lew's movie star blue eyes stared into hers. He sounded a little brisk
when he said, "So, you were telling me about this wedding. Is it small?"

She looked down at Lew's phone. "Huge. Most of the time they are
where I come from. It will be an affair to remember. It always is."

"This summer?" he asked.

"Yes. August. I'll be the maid of honor. Ashley and I have been
friends since kindergarten. I sat next to her the first day and she smiled.
She reminded me of that moment, in high school, and that I made her
feel less lonely. How do you ever say no to a friend like that?"

Lew's eyes softened for a moment. "That's nice."

The conversation made her think about all she had to lose, how
much Ashley had to lose, Sadie's parents had to lose, if this turned into
a cluster.

She tried to hear anything going on behind her. She felt like the
poker player with her back exposed.

"August is nice. Better than winter." Lew read a text and showed it
to her.

"Yes."

Robbery took place in South Dakota when he was working on the oil fields. The investigator, here to pick him up, says he's hot headed and involved with other assaults. Her finger sat poised above his phone as she read the text.

Lew said casually, "I was in a wedding last winter."

"Really." She wasn't much interested in anybody's wedding at the moment.

"My brother's."

Lew had a brother. Now she knew he had a grandfather with prostate cancer and a brother.

"I bet that was fun."

"My cousin, Louis, got drunk and cut off the tip of his finger, and we, the collective we, almost burned down the barn we were renting for the wedding."

She closed her eyes. His cousin's name was Louis Lew. The phone vibrated, and she almost dropped it.

Man he's with is somebody he met at the fields. Ex-con. Was in for robbery.

She looked up from the phone to see Lew's expression. He was staring at the man's back. Lew's left hand was below the table. She surmised that he had pulled his gun when he laughed loudly at the meme.

Sadie slid the phone back across the table when the meals came. She looked up into the face of her friend, Officer Lucy Tomczak.

"Can I get you anything else?"

"Looks great," Lew said.

"Perfect," Sadie added.

Lucy cleaned the bar with a towel.

"So, out of curiosity, what kind of guy would you take to a wedding?"

She blanked. It was a question she didn't have answer for. "I haven't thought about it."

Lew began moving his food around his plate. Stanley turned and looked at Lew and then at Lucy.

"Hey. Where's the other one?"

Lucy stopped cleaning. "What other one?"

"The other one. I'm not leaving you any tip."

Lucy smiled and dropped the towel on a table like she was a regular at the restaurant. "No worries, I didn't expect it."

"Where's our food?"

"Soon."

The man turned around again. Sadie watched Lucy, still cool as a cucumber. Lew watched the men. No one moved from their positions, as if stuck in a Hopper painting.

Suddenly, Stanley Kowal sat straight up. He was catching on, too late, that something had changed in the restaurant.

His partner was getting edgy as well. "We need to leave, Stan. Forget the food. I don't like this. Something's up."

"Shut it," Kowal growled.

Lew nodded slightly to his left, and Sadie stood quietly moving to her right. She turned and smiled politely as she faced the smaller man. She aimed her weapon at his chest. He lifted his arms slowly, linking his hands behind his head.

Kowal watched his friend, and after putting two and two together, stood instantly, almost improbably, considering his size. Lucy yelled orders at Stanley Kowal to get down on the floor.

The skinny partner looked uneasily from Lucy to Stanley. The giant remained resolute. Perhaps, always the bully, he believed he could force his way out of this situation, blunder his way forward as he had probably done most of his life.

Lew repeated the order Lucy had just given. He was loud and commanding. "Get down on the floor and put your arms out. I want to see your hands palm up, away from your body."

"Get out of my way!" Kowal yelled the words with the force of a violent hurricane. There was no running from his past, and he knew it.

Sadie could see the officers outside the front door ready to enter. Without raising her voice, she said, "As you can see, there are more officers outside, Mr. Kowal. I am not going to have you cause havoc in this fine establishment. You have been told to get down and to put your arms out, away from your side. I want you to do what you've been told without any more fuss."

He flinched when she said his name. "How do you know who I am?"

An officer came through the from the sandwich shop side, and another entered from the front door of the restaurant. The skinny partner threw himself to the floor, assuming the position.

Stanley Kowal stared at Sadie for a moment, then dropped heavily to the floor. Officer Lucy Tomczak patted down the suspect as Lew holstered his weapon and got down on his knees to help Lucy. Sadie lowered hers but kept it ready.

Lucy found nothing of any importance in his pockets. They cuffed Kowal and raised him, like a pillar, to a standing position. Someone dragged the small thin man up and away, like a battered sheet in the wind.

Investigator O'Bannon walked in wearing his flak jacket over his crisp white shirt and nodded a hello. Another plain clothes officer, a man she didn't know, was with him. The man read Stanley Kowal his rights. He was under arrest for robbery and attempted murder of a man named Clifford Jones, in the town of Buffalo, South Dakota. Sadie looked at the officer's cowboy hat and his cowboy boots and the gray-blond hair. He tipped his hat to them as he and a US marshal moved the behemoth through the door. A little paperwork, and they'd be gone.

KHAO SOI

Recipe from Chef Joe Hatch-Surisook of Sen Yai Sen Lek in Northeast Minneapolis, Minnesota

Serves 4

Ingredients

2 tablespoons oil

1 pound stew beef, cut into 1-inch cubes

4½ cups water

2 14-ounce cans coconut milk

5 cloves garlic, chopped

1 shallot, sliced

1 4-ounce can red curry paste

1½ tablespoons yellow curry powder

½ teaspoon turmeric

6+ tablespoons fish sauce

5 tablespoons sugar

3+ tablespoons tamarind concentrate

Salt, to taste

1½ pounds fresh thin egg noodles

Oil for frying

Garnish ingredients:

Green onion, chopped

Cilantro leaves

Shallots, sliced

Limes, cut into wedges

Pickled Chinese mustard greens, sliced

Thai chili powder

Directions

1. Heat 2 tablespoons oil in a Dutch oven or heavy bottomed mediumsized pot over high heat. Add beef and brown or sear on all sides, approximately 3–4 minutes.

Add water, bring to a boil, lower heat and simmer, covered, 45 minutes to 1 hour or until tender. Remove beef with slotted spoon and reserve beef stock.

2. Skim 1–1½ cups coconut cream from cans of coconut milk and have it ready. Set aside remaining coconut milk and cream.

3. In a Dutch oven or heavy bottomed mediumsized pot over high heat (you can use the same beef pot after stock has been reserved), add the 1–1½ cups of coconut cream, garlic, and shallots. Stir fry for 30 seconds. Add curry powder, curry paste, and turmeric. Cook until bubbling, stirring occasionally, approximately 1 minute.

4. Add beef, remaining coconut milk, and reserved beef stock. Bring to a boil, lower heat, and add fish sauce, sugar, and tamarind concentrate. Taste for flavor balance. Turn off heat or allow to gently simmer.

5. Fill a deep, heavy bottomed pot, pan, or wok with approximately 1½ inches of oil and heat to 350 degrees F.

6. Take ½ pound of noodles, shake them out, and in small handfuls add to hot oil and fry until crispy, turning once, approximately 10–15 seconds. Remove with slotted spoon and drain on paper towel. Do this in batches until complete.

7. Cook the remaining 1 pound of noodles in boiling water until done, approximately 1–2 minutes. Drain and rinse with cold water.

8. Portion out noodles into bowls and ladle curry over noodles.

9. Top with fried noodles and garnish with green onion, cilantro leaves, shallots, limes, pickled Chinese mustard greens, and Thai chili powder.

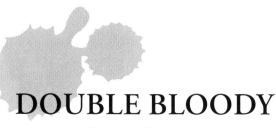

DOUBLE BLOODY

By Amy Pendino

JOEL SHOVED HIS key into the back door's lock, but the deadbolt had already been turned. Six-fifteen in the morning, and someone had left the restaurant wide open. He mentally ticked through last night's activities: who was on duty, what parties were hosted, which manager was scheduled to close. Niya. Niya would have been in charge last night, but everyone at the Firehouse knew her to be meticulous about following her procedures, so he was sure things were put to rights before she left. She would have locked the back door when she went home.

His was the first car in the parking lot that Sunday morning. Last night's freezing rain had been followed by a few inches of sodden snow, and tire tracks marked the surface like a kindergartner's art project. One set of tracks continued past the lot's edge, up and over a snowbank before bashing against a huge snow pile the road grader had left behind.

Joel straightened his shoulders and stepped into the kitchen. Silence met his careful breaths: nothing hummed, dripped, or bubbled. A computer monitor from the office sent out undulating red, yellow and orange waves in shimmering arcs like flames that danced over the concrete floor and made dark, angular shadows in the corners. From the doorway, at least, nothing looked out of place.

Tiny, peek-through slits in the big swinging doors, which led into the dining area, weren't large enough to let in more than gauzy blue light, and Joel knew he needed to check the dining area beyond them. He crossed over to one and peeked through: the eating area, still robed in darkness, was still. All of the high tops were set, all stools and chairs waited in their places, menus were neatly stacked at the hostess stand, and the floor appeared swept and clean. Satisfied, Joel turned back to the office.

He dropped his backpack onto the office floor and hung his leather flight jacket on a plastic hook above it. Snapping on the overhead light, he turned to the desk and saw that the schedules folder and the folder of purchase orders were both open, their contents spread across the desktop like they'd been dropped and discarded. The left side desk drawer was ajar, half of the files inside hanging awkwardly like a hard wind had swept through them. The metal lockbox used for small bills had been wrenched open, but the money was still inside. Obviously, Joel thought, he'd need to do a more thorough walk-through. But first, he called 9-1-1.

He'd worked so long in food service that he was used to the odors that clung to restaurant walls—Firehouse made its burgers from organic beef bought from a farmer just down the road—but the aroma that seeped into Joel's awareness as he entered the dining room was more coppery, more acidic, than the remains of last night's dinners.

He swerved into the U-shaped bar area to flip on the main room's overhead lights. When his left foot slipped, he reached out to steady himself, banging his wrist on the marble countertop. He regained his balance, cursing and rubbing his wrist before fumbling again for the lights. They illuminated the center of the cavernous dining area like a brilliant spotlight in a circus tent. Joel stopped himself from taking another step, the obscene display before him snatching his attention: a red pulpy stain, smeared across the stainless steel serving counter, puddled down the front of the counter into dark pitchy blots between the webs of the floor's rubber matting. Large scarlet droplets decorated the front of the stainless steel refrigerator. The sticky mess curled out from the bar's flooring into the first seating area like something had been dragged to the adjacent section, the area reserved for parties and today's brunch.

Joel's stomach dropped. He barely reached the small sink before retching his morning coffee into the drain. Bracing himself there, his throat burning and mind racing, he fought against the wracking heaves that swept through his body. What the hell had happened last night?

· · · · ·

The former Firehouse was a bar on the main drag that served pizza and 3.2 beer. Locals could get the pizza delivered but not the beer. Then one of the owners passed away, and since he was the guy who made the pizzas, all the Firehouse had left to offer was cheap beer and conversation.

Most of the gents who perched on the stools sipped Bud and kept up a steady flow of feed prices and farm gossip. And then the place burned down. The last owner left, deciding to move to Florida instead of rebuilding.

For the next few years, nothing new appeared in town to replace the lost restaurant. Neighbors drove to Webster for their 3.2, but the bar there didn't serve food unless pickled eggs and meat sticks could be counted as elements of a healthy diet. As a point of interest, the same old farmers who frequented the former Firehouse also ran the local township meetings, held the first Tuesday of every month. They made decisions about money for road maintenance and keeping the ballpark lights on. They also approved or rejected applications to buy or build businesses within the township boundaries. On this last topic, their lips were tighter than a fish's. The only way the townspeople knew something new had been approved was when a backhoe was hauled over to Peterson's side pasture, the one that ran along County Road 2. A big hole formed there over the course of a few afternoons. After that, a square brick building crept up from the foundation, a few feet higher each day. The new structure had a squat roof but nice skylight windows around the top. A covered entryway and a smooth parking lot completed the project.

For months after the construction debris disappeared, the place looked finished from the outside but remained as quiet and dark as could be. Then, early one spring afternoon, a big flatbed backed into the parking lot and off rolled shiny silver appliances wrapped in clear plastic. Cardboard signs popped up on residential street corners next to the stop signs most drivers rolled through. "Firehouse Grille, Opening in April!" the placards announced, orange and yellow flames decorating the letters.

The locals talked about this after mass, when most everybody went down the hill to Helen's Café for coffee before heading home. A surprise announcement caused a major stir when Helen shared her decision to close the café. She was tired of being on her feet all day every day, she said. As soon as the new Firehouse opened, she was heading down South to live with her sister. And she "didn't give a rip" about what would happen to the collection of fabric, metal, and ceramic chickens she'd used as decoration inside her café; as far as she was concerned, someone could plant 'em on the front lawn of the new restaurant.

The new Firehouse opened before school let out for the summer. Cate and Gregg, the owners, made it a priority to greet and visit with every guest. Cate's bouncy sparkle made even the most dour farmers grin. Her husband, Gregg, remembered every patron's name and favorite beer. People said they could tell the Larssons had previous restaurant experience: the burgers arrived fast and hot, the wait staff was perky but not overly friendly, and the bill could be settled without an annoying request to take a look at the dessert tray first.

Compared to the old Firehouse, the décor inside the new place was also much improved: though both sported the same theme, Gregg and Cate took care to find authentic equipment actually used to fight fires once upon a time. Old wooden ladders crisscrossed the vaulted ceiling, and old fire hoses wrapped the exposed joists overhead. Worn boots, helmets, and firemen's jackets posed in the corners, and above the hostess stand rested a child's pedal fire truck from decades ago. One tiny chicken, wearing a fire helmet, roosted in the truck's seat in homage to the town's former café owner.

After only a few months, the Firehouse Grille showed itself to be a success. A staff of nineteen waited tables, six high school kids worked the hostess stand and folded napkins when they weren't seating diners, and three cooks rotated through the weekly menu specials according to each one's particular specialty. The biggest improvement was that the new restaurant won township approval to host a full bar, including the new spirits with fancy names created in local and small distilleries around the state.

The most popular weekly special was celebrated each Sunday. After the brunch items were cleared and the long buffet tables had been taken down, the Firehouse hosted what came to be known as "The Twin Cities' Best Bloody Mary Bar." A bartender from California accepted a six-month contract to establish the weekly event and train the other bartenders in the secrets and nuances of his recipes and their creative, delicious variations. He based the unusual modifications—a yellow Mary, for example, with yellow veggies and pepper vodka, or a spicy version with Sriracha—on a simple recipe that he mixed every Monday at a catering kitchen in Saint Paul. This recipe, using only bottles of vodka he distilled with garlic, remained Rick's secret, one he guarded from everyone except the Firehouse's owners who had recruited him and paid him generously to share his expertise and mixing magic. He said he'd leave the recipe with Cate and Gregg when his contract expired.

· · · · ·

The Saturday night before Joel found the Firehouse Grille in disarray, there was a glitch. The weekly menu schedule had to be changed unexpectedly. Instead of the prime rib special the locals were used to ordering before their movies in Lakeville or their Netflix back home, diners were forced to choose between a sirloin steak with baby red potatoes or a vegan alternative with smashed cauliflower that went entirely unordered. The restaurant's beef supplier had been called away and couldn't deliver their regular order of prime rib before he left.

This change upset many diners, especially the older ones. True Minnesotans, no one spoke of their displeasure to the staff, but murmurs of "well, that's that, then" or "wouldn't'cha know" whistled between seatmates. Every table was taken, but the usual Saturday night clamor was subdued. Niya, who had her own serving section, also acted as hostess because Trina was at a school dance and forgot to find a sub. The new bartender was having a tough time keeping up, so she also helped him when she could.

Niya was racing back to the kitchen when she spied Rick, the Bloody Mary expert, at the back door, holding plastic baggies of chopped veggies he'd prepared for Sunday's event. "Rick! Are you free to help out?" Niya balanced a stack of dirty plates on one arm. "The new bartender's good, but he's not real fast. We could use you, just for an hour."

Rick lowered his eyelids and blew out a noisy breath. "Depends." His response oozed out as if he had all the time in the world to answer.

Niya dropped her plates into a tub next to the dishwasher, wiped her hands along her apron, and perched her fists on her hips. "What the heck, Rick? Your contract's for six more weeks, right?"

"Right," the dark-haired man drawled, elongating the "i" like a bratty teenager. He clenched his jaw, stuck out his dimpled chin, and tapped those fancy leather boots he liked to wear even when working.

Niya rolled her eyes. "Get on up to the bar then. Help us out a little. Can you whip up a few Bloodies for a late-night happy hour?"

Rick's eyes opened. "You can't tell me what to do. My schedule's for Gregg and Cate, not you. You're just a—"

She interrupted. "They're out of town at a wedding. They left me in charge tonight. And I'm asking—no, I'm telling you—mix some drinks before you head home. It's not that hard." She stormed back into the dining area without waiting for his reply.

The dishwasher had stopped loading and was watching their exchange like a gamer glued to his screen. Even Mike, the languorous Saturday chef with the "man bun" and the rainbow hairnet, lingered to see what the famous bartender would do next.

Rick removed his coat, peeling off one sleeve at a time, then folded and placed it onto the office chair. He adjusted the collar of his white button-up shirt before unrolling and rebuttoning the cuffs of his sleeves. Then he sashayed past them through the swinging door in an exaggerated imitation of the exit Niya had executed ahead of him.

Chef Mike met the dishwasher's eyes, shrugged, and turned back to the fry pad.

Back in the dining area, a crowd of customers waited at the hostess stand while Niya took an order from the booth on the far left. Two little kids who should have been home in bed clambered across the table between their parents, who ignored their misbehavior and discussed their second menu choices. Rick strode into the U-shaped bar and placed both manicured hands on its marble top. To his left sat two regulars in their tan Carhartt coats and seed caps, nursing beers so light they looked almost clear. To his right were three ladies dressed, made up, and perfumed for their night out, the Firehouse being their first stop. They weren't interested in food and were taking selfies as they waited to order drinks. Directly in front of Rick sat an older man, silver-haired, his deep tan not quite disguising the many wrinkles on his face and neck. He wore a V-necked sweater over a pink shirt.

"What'll you have?" Rick's tone exuded impatience.

"You the new owner?"

Rick checked to see that the novice bartender's attention was somewhere else. A smile broke across his chiseled jaw. He stood tall and folded his arms across his chest. "Yes. Yes, I am," he lied. Dishonesty wasn't a foreign practice to him.

"Quite the changes, huh? And that Bloody Mary thing? Wow," the older guy gushed. "Great idea. I owned the old Firehouse, you know," he added. "Looking at this place, I kinda wish I'd stuck around."

"Good to meet you." Rick held out his hand, shook with the older man, then wiped his palm with the bar rag. "Interesting you should stop in tonight." Rick looked both ways and lowered his voice. "I'd like to sell this place and get into a more lucrative market. Maybe we could—"

Niya swept up to enter her food order into the computer.

"I'll be back," Rick spoke quietly. "I have an idea." He smiled; the even white tiles of his teeth gleamed.

Turning his attention to the three women on the other side, Rick didn't have to work hard to engage their interest. "We've got a little something we call 'Bloody Mary's Night Out,'" he told them. "It's like our popular Bloody, but I substitute tequila for the vodka. I add a little something extra too. Girls love it."

The green-eyed woman, the one with reddish lipstick on her top tooth, ordered for all three. They asked Rick to stand next to them and took more selfies while they held their drinks high and arranged themselves in ridiculous poses.

By the time Rick got back to the serving side of the bar, the tanned gentleman had disappeared.

"Can I interrupt you? I need these drinks." Niya was back. Her red cheeks showed her displeasure with Rick.

Rick snatched the paper order from her hand. "Why don't you use the computer for drinks like you do for food?" he snarled. "That's why this place is never going to be a first-class bar. Simple things, small fixes like this—"

"I'll do it myself," the waitress interrupted. There was something about Rick—the way he smirked, his declaration that the new Firehouse T-shirts should not be considered proper serving attire, even how he declined the other staff members' invitations to hang out after closing—something about the California bartender made Niya's patience run thin.

He stopped her entry into the bar area. "I've got this. Do your own job," Rick hissed, then tossed a wink to the three ladies witnessing the exchange.

Niya obliged, silently rehearsing the list of grievances against him that she planned to share with Cate when the owners got back.

Rick stayed at the Firehouse for another hour. He ignored the servers and pretended not to hear Mike's "good night" when he left, banging the door shut behind him.

· · · · ·

THE FIRST OFFICER to arrive at the restaurant the next morning was the newest hire for New Market Township. She walked Joel back to his truck, thanked him for sharing his observations, and sent him home with instructions to contact the owners. After calling in the situation and asking for a medical examiner, she reentered the kitchen and took pictures with her phone of the area and appliances.

Then she looked into the office, noticed the disorder, and took some time to peruse the notes, scheduling requests, invoices, and other papers discarded on the desktop. One folder was closed and pushed to the far side; the name "Rick Daniels" was inked on its tab. The short side of a white paper index card peeked out.

The officer stood back for a moment and listened before deciding she was the only one in the restaurant. Taking a breath, she stepped forward again and used a pencil eraser to open the folder. A copy of the contract between Rick and the owners of the Firehouse was on the top of a pile of papers. At the bottom, a handwritten note had been added: *This contract is terminated as of December 6.* Five days from today, she noted. It was signed by both Gregg Larsson and Rick Daniels. She took a photo of it. Under that were Rick's professional résumé and a collection of three-by-five recipe cards. She started flipping through them but quit when she heard the back door squeal open.

Closing the folder, she slid it back to its previous location. She left the office and entered the bar area where she took photos of the garish stains and puddles, following the blood trail which swept around the bar to one of the tall vertical ceiling columns: there rested an untidy coil of old rope. A splotch of red tinged the loops nearest to her feet.

An angry voice rang out from the back, interrupting the officer's inspection. "I'm the owner. What's going on here?"

She met him at the swinging doors, recognizing him despite her short tenure on the force. "Mr. Larsson? I was told you were out of town." She raised her arms, but he looked past her into the dining area.

"Oh my God, is that blood?" He placed one hand over his mouth, his voice subdued.

The county sheriff arrived just behind him and turned the man by his shoulders. "Gregg, we can't have you in here just now." His words were gentle as he steered the owner away from the scene. "Can we get you to answer a few questions outside?"

She thought they'd gone but heard them in the office. Gregg was trying to persuade the sheriff to let him stay. "But I can access the video here. We should be able to see on here what . . . who . . ." At the office threshold, the officer stood on her toes to see over the sheriff's shoulder.

While they examined the security tape inside, Niya's Honda slid to a stop at the edge of the restaurant's parking lot. One police vehicle, parked at an angle across the lot entrance, prevented access; another was in the far corner next to a snowbank where it looked like an officer was inspecting the icy mound. Niya could see yellow crime scene tape crossing the restaurant's front door. She parked as close as she could and got out of the car. "Excuse me, Officer, I work here. Is there any way I can get in?"

"Nope. Property's secured. No one in nor out."

"It's just that I have some information." Niya rubbed her fingers across her forehead. "Can you get a message to the owner? I think he's inside."

The officer's sunglasses covered his eyes though the day was gray and overcast. "Sorry, can't do that. Can't you call him?"

Niya shook her head. "He's not answering. Neither is the bartender, Rick. The thing is, I went by the bartender's apartment before I came here. His car's gone, and the guy who lives across the hall said he saw Rick dragging two big suitcases to his car late last night. He asked Rick if he was moving." She swallowed. "Rick laughed and said he got a better offer."

The officer thought for a moment. "Come with me, but don't touch nothing."

Niya and the officer entered the restaurant as the others came out from the office.

Gregg reached out and the two met in a hug.

"Joel called me. He must've reached you too. What happened?" she asked.

"There was some sort of fight here last night."

"Between who? Who else has keys to get in?"

"Rick was definitely part of it." Gregg explained what they'd been able to glean from the video. "I recognized his boots."

"You said a fight. Was someone hurt?"

"Two men dressed in hooded sweatshirts came into the restaurant last night after closing," he said. "Rick and somebody else. We can't see who is who. Plus, the damn audio didn't work."

The sheriff directed them outside and finished the story on the sidewalk. "After they fought, one of 'em tied the other up and the other guy disappeared from the video for a while. He came back with a handful of papers and note cards. He carried the other guy out when he left."

"Sheriff?" Their conversation was interrupted by the officer who'd been working at the snowbank. "I got some info on that license plate, the one that banged into that snow pile, I mean. It's from Florida. The tag was etched in reverse in the ice."

"Call it in and get a BOLO started for that car." He put a black watch cap on. The wind had picked up, blowing ice shards off the little trees planted in the restaurant's courtyard. "We need to clear out and get the property released." Turning to Gregg, he added, "I'll let you know what develops."

· · · · ·

A white Cadillac with Florida plates was pulled over by a Missouri State patrolman a few hours later. Rick Daniels, at the wheel, gave the patrolman a false name before claiming that he'd borrowed the car, registered to the former Firehouse owner. The body of the older man was found in the trunk, along with twelve bottles of vodka, plastic bags holding a variety of chopped vegetables, and a white three-ring binder that contained recipes for a variety of Bloody Mary mixes.

The suspect, awaiting his preliminary hearing, says he misjudged the former owner's offer to buy his recipes and all future rights to their use. He also admits that he may have misled the man into believing that he was the owner of the new Firehouse Grille and would be interested in selling it, causing a disagreement that escalated into the bloody fight captured on tape. The suspect maintains his innocence, says the killing was accidental, and blames the misunderstanding on the subtle nuances of Minnesota speech patterns which, in his opinion, are impossible to interpret correctly.

The Firehouse Grille has reopened and now serves Bloody Mary cocktails using only the traditional recipe.

FIREHOUSE BLOODY MARY

This base recipe is used as is, or can be altered in a variety of ways (two included):

Prep vodka mix: Add 3 tablespoons of minced garlic to a bottle of vodka; steep for 3 days; strain and relabel bottle.

Basic mix:

3 cans Clamato

1 bottle Pickapeppa Sauce

½ bottle Worcestershire sauce

1 tablespoon horseradish

20 dashes Tabasco sauce

Few dashes of pepper

Directions

For individual serving, mix 1 ounce of vodka mix with 4 ounces of basic mix.

Garnish rim of glass with salt and pepper.

Add celery stalk, pickle, ½ stick Slim Jim, skewer of cubed mozzarella and cheddar cheeses.

VARIATIONS

Yellow Mary: Substitute Absolut "pepper" for vodka. Change basic mix to the following:

1 liter yellow tomato juice

6 ounces yellow bell pepper juice

6 ounces pineapple juice

4 ounces mango juice

6 tablespoons lemon juice

1 teaspoon white pepper

Use same ratio of 1 ounce Absolut to 4 ounces Yellow Mary mix. Garnish rim with salt and pepper; add yellow bell pepper sticks to stir.

Spicy Mary: Substitute Sriracha for Tabasco in the basic recipe. Add buffalo wing, rosemary sprig, and a small tomato to stir.

CATCH OF THE DAY

By Marcia Adair

LAKE SUPERIOR SPARKLED like a million diamonds in the late June sunshine. As Libby McFee drove her rusty old Subaru along its North Shore, she gazed at the treasure wistfully.

A million diamonds, she thought. *Wouldn't that just solve everything.* Highway 61 hummed beneath her bald tires as she pondered her woes—newly divorced, no money, and a mortgage in foreclosure. All thanks to her ex, Jake McFee.

Her mother had warned her about the handsome, mustachioed charmer. "He's a scammer, honey. He's got a rap sheet. He'll ruin your life."

"But I *love* him. He'll *change*," Libby had countered with the impassioned confidence of youth. She wished she'd listened to her mother.

Painful memories washed over her, followed by waves of shame for having been such a naïve Nelly; next came the familiar flush of anger and the clenched jaw. Without realizing it, she was driving seventy-five miles per hour down the serpentine two-lane road along the cliff edge. Her thoughts careened just as recklessly into dangerous, satisfying fantasies of diamonds—and revenge.

She smirked at how insanely jealous Jake would be if she finally had something he couldn't take from her. How enraged he would be if she could make it without him. *If only there was a way,* she mused.

A soft woof from the backseat brought her back to the present. "Hey, Boondoggle. You hungry, boy? I bet you are. A week of camping will do that to ya." The black Lab thumped his tail enthusiastically, nearly knocking a pile of camping gear on the floor. A cooler of fresh-caught walleye rattled in the back.

"You know what? I am too. Let's give ourselves a little treat and stop by The Fish 'n' Game. Our buddy Mavis will cook up those walleyes for us."

Libby had been going to the campy café for thirty years, ever since she was a kid. Every visit to her grandparents' remote cabin near the far tip of Cook County included a swing by the quirky house-cum-restaurant.

Its claim to fame was that Mavis and her husband, Harold, would cook up any fish or game a customer brought in—or diners could order what the duo caught, hunted, or trapped. It was one of the few mom-and-pop places that still existed, although barely.

"Tourists these days . . ." Mavis had taken to saying with a touch of disdain. "All they want is to drive fast and find what they already have in the city. No one's looking for something original—especially a place that has woodchuck on the menu. I'm sixty-eight and widowed, Libby; how am I ever going to retire? This place is gonna be the death of me."

Ah, Mavis. We both have troubles, Libby thought. *But we always seem to make each other feel better, don't we? Hang on. I'll be there soon.* Cheered by having a cozy plan to wrap up her vacation, Libby focused on Minnesota's most scenic drive. She flipped on the radio in time to catch the end of the news.

". . . robbed a series of banks and businesses from the Twin Cities to Duluth. Both men are armed and considered dangerous. It is believed they are headed to Canada."

"Dang, Boo. Looks like we got out of the woods at the right time. I wouldn't want to run into those guys."

An hour later, Libby pulled into The Fish 'n' Game's gravel parking lot and switched off the engine. She wasn't surprised that the lot was empty—that was pretty much the case most days, Mavis had told her—but she raised a brow when she realized the OPEN sign wasn't in the window.

"Weird," Libby said to Boo. "Why would she be closed on a Friday at dinnertime during tourist season? I'm sure she'll open up for us, though, eh? We're practically family." Boo gave an eager woof, clearly happy to be at the familiar spot where he always got treats and ear scritches.

She got out and opened Boo's door. He bounded toward the porch but stopped short and gave an inquiring look to Libby. He ran around to the back of the building barking, returned to the steps leading up to the porch, and growled. Then he wagged his tail and laid down.

Libby watched in bemusement. "All right, squirrel brain. You wait out here 'til you settle down."

She took the four wooden porch steps two at a time, then peered in the windows. The dining room was empty. No surprise, given the vacant parking lot. Libby furrowed her brow. Why wasn't Mavis doing her sudoku at the front register like she always did when things were slow?

As she reached for the knob, Libby saw fresh gouge marks on the door jamb. The hair on the back of her neck prickled.

Thoughts of Mavis lying somewhere injured or worse flooded her mind. Heart racing, Libby opened the door slowly and peeked in. "Hello?"

A pallid, disheveled young man in his thirties shuffled his lanky frame out of the kitchen. He looked uncomfortable, arms crossed and rocking from foot to foot. An oversized gray T-shirt hung loose over his baggy jeans, completing the impression of a man resigned to defeat.

"Oh, um, hi," Libby ventured. "Are you open?"

"Am I what? Oh, you mean the restaurant?" He looked panicked, eyes wide and mouth dry, judging from the lip smacking. "Okay, sure, why not." He glanced around nervously and shook his long blond hair out of his eyes.

"Great. I'm starved," Libby replied, trying to sound casual and friendly. "I haven't been here for a while," she lied, "but I remember some sweet old lady who used to cook up the best walleye. Mabel somebody, was it? Is she around? I'd like to say hi."

The man looked like a deer in the headlights. Finally he blurted, "Oh, Granny Mabel? Um, yeah. She took a little . . . vacation. I'm helping out."

"How nice," she said. *Three strikes,* she thought. *The name was Mavis, not Mabel. She didn't have any children, let alone grandchildren. And she'd never take off at the height of tourist season.*

She spied a crude prison tattoo on his hand. Her ex had one like it: three dots, meaning "my crazy life."

Two robbers. Armed and dangerous. The news report she'd heard a few miles back played in her head.

Libby's heart thudded in her chest. Where was Mavis? And where was the other robber?

"You must be her daughter's son, the one in college in Duluth," she prattled. She wondered if he'd take the bait.

"Sure, whatever."

"I've forgotten your name."

"Gil," he blurted, clapping his hand over his mouth. Libby smiled encouragingly.

"Oh, yes, you're the one studying physiology, right?"

"Fizzy-what?" The man glanced toward the window. "Is that your dog barking out there? Why doesn't he shut up? He's making me nervous."

Libby looked out the window and listened more closely. Boo was doing the same confused running around, barking, growling, and wagging he'd done when they arrived. He knew something was wrong too.

"Are you gonna order something or what?" His voice was getting edgy. "And make that mutt shut his trap."

"No problem," Libby replied. "How about some walleye cakes for me and a bowl of water for my dog?"

"Fine," he said. "You can get the water yourself," he added, nodding toward a pitcher near the register.

Gil retreated to the kitchen. From the entry, Libby saw him rummaging through cupboards and drawers.

Walleye's in the refrigerator, you poser, she thought.

Libby tiptoed in behind him and slid a bowl off the shelf. Gil wheeled around nervously at the sound. "Stop sneaking around. Get out of here. You can't be in here."

"Sorry, it's for the dog. To make him stop barking." She backed away, keeping her eye on Gil and the chef's knives near his hand. That was when she spied a bullet hole in the back wall. A cast iron skillet lay on the floor next to a pool of blood.

She turned, snatched the pitcher, and rushed outside. She'd get the dog in the car and drive to the nearest phone.

"Boondoggle! Come!"

The dog loped toward her from behind the restaurant, tail wagging.

"C'mon, boy," she commanded. She headed toward the car, but the dog turned and ran back to where he'd come from.

Libby swore under her breath, dropped the pitcher, and followed at a run. She found Boo barking excitedly at the shed, tail wagging wildly, paws clawing insistently at the locked door. From inside came a low moan.

"Mavis! Are you all right?" She pounded on the door.

Another moan, deeper and more prolonged, escaped from the shed.

"Hang on, Mavis. I'll get you out of there." Libby dropped to her hands and knees to search through the tall grass for a rock, anything to smash the padlock. She didn't hear Gil come up behind her. He yanked her to her feet and spun her around.

"Get away from the shed."

"No. Not until I know Mavis is safe," Libby said defiantly. Boo growled protectively, then returned to his tail wagging at the shed door. "That's how Boo acts with people he knows and loves. I know you have her in there. I heard her moaning. I saw the bullet hole and the frying pan and the blood on the kitchen floor. If you've hurt her, I'll . . ."

"That's enough," he cut in. "You need to come with me. Now." Gil strong-armed her toward the café, shoved her inside, and slammed the door.

She spun around to face him. "You don't scare me," she lied. "I'm not backing down until I know Mavis is safe. She doesn't have grandkids. You don't know the first thing about running a restaurant. Mavis wouldn't leave this place in the summer. I know who you are. You're one of the two bank robbers I heard about on the radio. I saw the jimmied lock. What did you do to my friend?"

Before he could answer, Libby heard footsteps coming from the kitchen. Her head swam as she prepared to face the second robber. *Armed and dangerous.* The words ricocheted in her mind. Her breath came in shallower and shallower gulps.

A rifle barrel poked out of the kitchen.

Libby's knees turned to rubber, and her jaw dropped as the gunman emerged.

"Mavis?"

"Hi, Libby." Mavis smiled warmly and spoke calmly. She was wearing her trademark Kiss the Cook—Or Else apron. "Sorry I couldn't greet you when you first got here. I was out back checking on the other robber. I've got him tied up in the shed. By the time I came back in, you'd gone out." She waved her rifle in Gil's general direction. "I sent this guy out to get you so I could explain everything."

Libby wobbled over to the nearest chair and sat down.

Mavis let out a belly laugh. "Relax, girl. Everything's under control." She reached under the counter and pulled out a flask. She tossed it to Libby. "You better take a swig of this whiskey before you pass out, child."

"But I . . . I don't understand, Mavis," she sputtered between nips. "I saw the bullet hole in the wall and blood on the floor. I thought it was you moaning in the shed."

Mavis waved the rifle at Gil again and ordered him to sit on the floor behind the register. He complied.

"Well, it's like this," she began. "I was asleep upstairs and heard someone breaking in down here early this morning. Caught this idiot and his friend with their hands in the till. They were trying to rob my restaurant. Stealing from a little old widow lady. Tsk, tsk. Ever hear of such lowlifes?"

Gil cried, "*We're* lowlifes? You shot at *us*."

"Quiet," she commanded. "Anyway, I heard two armed robbers were headed north; I wanted to be ready for them. I guess they didn't count on me being a crack shot. They shoulda known a gal on her own is gonna be able to take care of herself. Ignoramuses didn't know Harold and I used to catch and hunt all the food for our menu. That's why we named this place The Fish 'n' Game, after all.

"Of course, I only wanted to scare the crappies out of them with Bessie." She laughed again, patting her thirty-aught-six. "Must have worked. One warning shot at the wall, and the taller guy stumbled backward. He reached for the stove to catch himself but fell and brought the skillet down on his own head. Dropped his gun and knocked himself out cold. Then this one put his hands up in surrender like I was a cop or something. I scooped up the handgun. It was great." She chuckled.

Gil grew indignant at the humiliating reminder. "That old bat is crazy. She made me drag my buddy to the shed and hogtie him. She shot out the tires in our car out back. And she's held me at gunpoint all day. Said if I tried to escape, my partner was toast."

"That got me to thinking," Mavis continued, ignoring Gil's outrage. "What's in all this aggravation for me? And it came to me."

"She said she'd shoot us dead if we didn't give her all the money from our heists," Gil blurted.

Libby gave Mavis an incredulous look. "Is that true? You're robbing the robbers?"

The woman shrugged impishly, and her eyes sparkled. "What can I say? Opportunity knocked. How could I say no? This break-in was the last straw. You know how long I've struggled to make this place succeed? I can't do it anymore, sweetie. I'm too old . . . and too sick."

"You're sick? What is it, Mavis?"

"I didn't want to worry you, hon; I've had a bad ticker for years. It's getting worse, they say. Doctors told me I'll be dead in three months if I don't stop working. But what am I supposed to do? I can't afford to retire, I can't make this place work, and no one wants to buy it. I figured taking their money was my chance to take care of myself before I check out. Who would ever know? And I'll be dead before they can prosecute me. Kinda seems like shooting fish in a barrel." She shrugged and gave Libby a wide-eyed innocent blink, as if her plan was the most logical thing in the world.

"Oh, Mavis." Libby's eyes teared up. "I had no idea. Is there anything I can do to help you?"

Mavis grinned. "Yeah, honey. Help me get the money from these clowns. You can have half. We'll both live like queens."

"What?" Libby's head was reeling. "Mavis, have you lost your mind? That's madness. It's . . ."

"Rather appealing?" Mavis suggested with another impish smile.

We'll live like queens. The words rolled in Libby's mind. What a change it would be from the financial struggles Jake had saddled her with. For a moment, Libby let her fantasies run wild. With all that money, Mavis could retire; Libby could save her home from foreclosure, maybe even quit her dead-end job. Libby melted into the reverie. It was almost as good as a million diamonds. Mavis was right: Who would know? It would solve all of their problems.

She beamed, but a cloud soon shadowed her face. "But what would we do with Frick and Frack here?"

"Ooh, we could cook 'em up. Harold has a great recipe for large game," Mavis deadpanned.

Gil gasped, eyes wide.

Libby suppressed a laugh. "Hmm. We could, but didn't you get rid of that large stew pot?"

"You're right, darn it."

Gil looked slightly relieved.

"But you could use two medium size ones."

He blanched.

They continued their banter, keeping a solemn tone, playing their fish until their captive was nearly exhausted.

Mavis got ready to reel him in. "Now where did you say that money was, Gil?" Mavis asked, aiming the rifle at his chest. "Last time I'm asking."

"It's at . . . it's in . . . No. No, I can't tell you. Stash will kill me, worse than you."

"Stash?" Libby asked.

Gil thrust out a defiant chin. "The guy in the shed. I ain't telling you his real name. And make that stupid mutt stop barking."

Libby realized Boo was still outside, running endless loops between the shed and restaurant. She smacked the heel of her hand to her forehead.

How could I have been so blind? she thought.

Without a word to the others, she strode to the phone on the counter, picked up the receiver, and dialed.

"What do you think you're doing?" Mavis demanded. "Who are you calling?"

"9-1-1. What is your emergency?" came the voice on the other end of the line.

"You know those two robbers the police have an alert out for? I have them here—at The Fish 'n' Game Café on Highway 61. One's in the restaurant; one's in the shed. Gil Somebody and Jake McFee."

Libby could scarcely hear the dispatcher over Mavis's and Gil's shouts.

"How'd you know his name?"

"Your *ex?*"

"Ma'am?" asked the dispatcher, hearing the cacophony of voices. "Are you okay? Are you safe? What is your location?"

Libby stuck her finger in her left ear to drown out Mavis and Gil as she gave the address of the restaurant. "I'm fine. And I know where the money is hidden too," she added. "I'll tell the officers when they arrive." She hung up despite the dispatcher asking her to stay on the line.

"Cops are on their way," she said.

"You better start explaining, Libby McFee," Mavis glowered. "You just blew my retirement plan."

"You're not a criminal, Mavis. Neither am I. Even if we could get away with it."

Chastened, Mavis paused and shifted gears. "Okay, okay. You gonna explain how you know it's your ex out in the shed? And how you know where the money is?"

Libby took a deep breath while Mavis kept the hunting rifle trained on Gil. "Boo and Gil told me it was Jake."

"I did not!" Gil protested.

"Hush. Boo tried to tell me right away. All that barking and tail wagging—he was telling me he knew who was in the shed. I thought it was you, Mavis. But when I knew you were safe, I figured he must've been barking at a raccoon or something.

"It was you, though, Gil, who tipped me to Jake. First, I noticed right away that you have the same prison tattoo my ex has. It's common enough; it didn't mean much at first. But you called him Stash. He got that name in prison—partly for how good he was at hiding things he'd stolen, partly for that cheesy moustache he's always had. I knew you'd been in lock up with him. Musta hitched your wagon to his latest star."

Gil slumped his shoulders and hung his head, the picture of total defeat.

Mavis looked impressed. "I guess I'm glad you never brought him by here. But how do you know where Stash stashed the cash?"

"You've known me since I was kid, Mavis. Remember when my family would come through here on our way to my grandparents' cabin?"

Mavis nodded. "The one out in the boonies by the Canadian border—right where these two were headed?"

"Exactly. The place is abandoned now, but Jake and I had checked it out in the past. He must have scouted it for a hideout and been hiding the money there. One more way he's tried to use me. And now it's coming back on him. Finally, he's going to pay for messing with me. Justice feels good."

Sirens in the distance shrieked louder as a squadron of police cars rushed into the parking lot. Two officers went directly to the shed, two more came into the restaurant, and the rest fanned out to assess and secure the area.

The two who came into the restaurant immediately relieved Mavis of her rifle and cuffed Gil.

Libby and Mavis recapped the events of the past twelve hours, getting to the part about the cabin hideaway as they watched officers hustle a handcuffed Jake to a patrol car.

Libby stepped outside to make sure he'd see her, know it was her who'd brought him down.

When he saw her, his mouth gaped. "Libby? What are you . . ."

Then it hit him. "Oh, man, is this that fish place you always talked about? I didn't know, Libs. I didn't. I swear."

For once, she believed him. It was the one treasure she hadn't shared with him.

Mavis joined her on the porch, followed by the officers and a dejected Gil as he headed to jail. "I told him we had enough money," he kept muttering. "I told him. But no. 'Just one more job,' he kept saying."

As one of the officers headed down the steps, he turned to Libby. "One more thing, ma'am," he said. "Because of the bank heist, the FBI has a reward out for these thieves. You two stand to make a pretty penny—even more from the bank and other businesses if your tip on the location of the stolen money pans out. Thanks again for your assistance."

As Libby and Mavis watched them drive away, they turned to each other and hugged, speechless with joy. Boo ran happy, noisy circles around them.

They turned and walked back inside. "We're a couple of rich single gals now," Mavis said, already spending the reward money ten times over in her mind. "Let's both retire and travel the world for a year. We'll go to London first, and from there . . ."

Libby didn't have the heart to tell her the reward wouldn't cover all her dreams. It would, however, give her enough money to hire help at The Fish 'n' Game and for Libby to get her house out of foreclosure.

"How about this for starters?" Libby smiled. She took a Sharpie from the front desk and went over to Mavis's OPEN sign: "Gone Fishin'" she scrawled over it in big, bold letters, and stuck the sign in the window.

"C'mon, Mavis. Jake and Gil aren't the only fish we caught. Let's fry up that batch of walleye I have in the cooler. We've got a lot to celebrate."

MANGO WALLEYE

Made by Chef Honorio Valencia, Tavern on Grand, Saint Paul, Minnesota

One grilled walleye, topped with a mango cilantro mix, served on a bed of wild rice and asparagus.

MANGO SALSA

Mix together:

4 cups diced mangos

2 ounces honey

2 diced red peppers

2 tablespoons lemon juice

1 bunch of cilantro

2 tablespoons orange juice

1 jalapeño diced

Salt and white pepper to taste

Plating

1 portion of wild rice

6 asparagus spears—sautéed in butter, salt, and pepper

Place asparagus on the bottom, then add the wild rice. Take 1 grilled walleye fillet and cut in half lengthwise and lay on top of the wild rice, then top with the mango salsa.

KILLER TACOS

By Chris Norbury

MAIJA SPRINKLED CABBAGE-HABANERO garnish on the fish taco she was assembling, drizzled it with creamy taco sauce, and handed it to her best friend and roommate, Claire. Their apartment was redolent with savory aromas: fresh herbs, spices, tacos, carnitas, tamales, and salsas. Maija was preparing a veritable Mexican smorgasbord for a dinner party that night. But her thoughts were of another kitchen in a different place: a professional kitchen in her own restaurant.

After Claire took a bite, Maija said, "What do you think?"

"Mmm." Claire swallowed and wiped sauce from her lips. "These are money, girlfriend. You *gotta* give the restaurant biz a try *now* before you chicken out."

"Thanks, but my inheritance from Abuela Sofia plus a loan from my parents still isn't enough."

"I say strike while the windfall is hot."

Maija shook her head. "The primary reason restaurants fail is undercapitalization. I've researched the heck out of that aspect of the business. Even with enough startup cash, my chances of success are only 20 percent."

Claire lifted an eyebrow. "Got any savings?"

Maija formed a *zero* with her fingers.

"What about a bank loan?"

"*Pfft*. Maybe at a double-digit interest rate."

Claire gave her a penetrating stare. "What does your heart tell you?"

Maija sighed. "I'm going crazy at work. Sure, data analysis pays the bills, but I'll die from boredom if I don't get out."

"And . . .?"

"If I don't try, Grammy Sofia's ghost will haunt me forever."

Claire's expression changed to impatience. "But . . .?"

"But I want to have enough money to give it my *best* shot."

After staring at the ceiling with a pensive expression, Claire said, "I've got some savings."

Maija gaped at her. "I can't ask you to risk your money on *me*."

Claire grasped her shoulders. "*I'm* asking *you* to *let* me, Blondie."

Maija stifled a protest. Claire had only uttered that hated nickname to emphasize her point. Thanks to her Finnish father and Mexican mother, Maija was an uncommon blonde-haired, blue-eyed Latina. She regretted not inheriting her mother's dark hair if only to avoid the incessant blonde jokes.

Maija searched Claire's eyes for sincerity. "Are you sure?"

"We'll work together." Claire smiled. "When *we* succeed, *we* share the profits."

Maija gaped again. "You want to *work* with me too?"

Claire, an elementary schoolteacher, nodded. "Weekends until summer vacation. Then full time. That'll save on labor." She walked to the dining room to lay out the silverware, then returned to the kitchen. "Hey, does the restaurant need to be a brick-and-mortar building?"

"Well, *duh*. Aren't all restaurants brick-and-mortar?"

"What about a food truck?"

"Seriously?"

"A used food truck's gotta be cheaper than a small restaurant."

"Hmm, I never considered that option. Grammy's bequest only said, 'Share your culinary gift with the world.' I assumed she wanted me to open a restaurant."

Maija's grandmother, Sofia Sanchez, had filled Maija's childhood with vivid, romantic stories about restaurant life decades ago back in Mexico. She and her husband had scrimped, saved, worked eighteen-hour days, and eventually built a successful chain of six restaurants across Baja California.

Under Sofia's tutelage, young Maija developed impressive culinary skills. She assumed the family cooking chores at age thirteen. Regrettably, she bowed to parental expectations after high school, abandoned her dream of culinary school, and got a "good job." Now, nearly thirty, she was terrified she'd end up settling for a dull, dead-end career pushing paper in small-town southern Minnesota. A food truck just might turn her dream into a reality. Excited, afraid, and apprehensive, Maija leveled a determined stare at Claire. "Let's go for it, *partner.*"

· · · · ·

They began to develop a business plan the next day. A week later, Maija got a phone call that solidified her decision. She clicked off and yelled, "I found a food truck."

"What?" Claire emerged from her bedroom. "How?"

"A friend of a friend. It's pretty beat up, but the kitchen's decent. My dad's mechanic checked it out. The engine's okay, but the brakes'll need work sooner rather than later. Most importantly, it's affordable."

"That was fast, you wheeler-dealer. I wouldn't know where to start looking."

Maija ordered two colorful plastic banners printed with their chosen business name, Cocina Divina, for the sides of the truck. The loose translation was *Heavenly Kitchen.* By the end of May, they'd cleaned and stocked the truck, passed the health department inspection, and obtained the necessary permits. Claire asked a teaching colleague, Zoie, who was a webmistress on the side, to set up a website and social media accounts so they could post their daily location.

For Cocina Divina's maiden voyage, Maija hoped she'd found a hidden gem—Straight River, Minnesota. A fifteen-minute drive from home. Several large businesses and factories in town. Host to many regional events that drew substantial crowds. The clincher? The city contained only one Mexican restaurant.

After a long last day at her old job, plus hours of final preparations for the food truck with Claire, Maija plopped onto the sofa, exhausted.

"Are we crazy?" she said. "Our money's almost gone. If we don't do enough business—"

"Relax, kiddo," Claire interrupted as she leaned back in the recliner. "Have faith in your talent."

Maija sighed. "You're right. What could go wrong?" Despite her words, she headed to bed expecting to have nightmares about their first day.

· · · · ·

Cocina Divina's opening weekend, at a softball tournament in Straight River, was a qualified success. Maija's food got raves, particularly from the owners of the local Chinese takeout place and the all-day diner who'd stopped by to wish them luck. But sales receipts didn't entirely offset the cost of the free samples they handed out.

The big challenge came on the third day when they parked near the biggest factory in town. Generating enough business from two lunch breaks and crossover traffic between shifts could jumpstart a torrent of positive buzz. To Maija's surprise, they fed more customers than they'd served each weekend day.

Back home that night, Claire said, "Girl, you're rockin' that town. Did you *see* those happy faces feasting on fresh, organic, authentic Mexican cuisine? Also, Zoie texted me. We now have well over one hundred followers on social media."

Maija's heart swelled as Abuela Sofia's spirit enveloped her like a warm hug.

· · · · ·

The next day, they worked a cluster of office buildings and light manufacturing shops. The lunch rush was their busiest yet. As the shift-change traffic wound down, Maija noticed a tall, beefy man with gray hair and a sizable gut standing nearby, arms folded, studying Cocina Divina. A younger man stood next to him, toeing the ground.

After the customer at the window had been served, both men stepped forward. The older man said, "New in town?"

Maija smiled. "Yes. This is our first week in business."

"That so?" Seemingly unimpressed, he inhaled the spicy, meaty, peppery aromas wafting outward from the truck, blown by the fan Maija had set up. Nodding toward the menu board, he slowly said, "Co-*sin*-ah Duh-*vin*-ah, eh?"

His attempt at Spanish pronunciation sounded clumsy and condescending. Was he mocking the blonde, blue-eyed *chica* who dared to sell Mexican cuisine from a run-down old food truck?

"Close enough," Maija said, and hesitantly corrected his pronunciation in rusty but serviceable Spanish. "Co-*seen*-ah Dee-*veen*-ah." She slid the sample plate forward. "Have a taste."

The man looked down his nose at the small paper cups, each filled with half a taco—fish, steak, or chicken. He picked up a fish taco, tossed it into his mouth, chewed, swallowed. Poker-faced, he locked eyes with Maija. "This gonna be a one-shot deal?"

She shook her head. "I plan to come back for the foreseeable future."

He flashed a too-perfect, megawatt smile. "Well then, welcome to Straight River. Name's Jim Baker. Everybody calls me Big Jim." He nodded toward the younger man. "My son, Johnny."

Johnny was chewing the second of two taco samples he'd taken, culinary bliss on his face, so he flapped his hand in greeting and mumbled something unintelligible.

"Thanks, Big Jim. I'm Maija Rantala. This is my business partner, Claire Kennedy."

Claire waved a soapy hand at him from the sink.

Big Jim said, "We own El Toro over on Main Street."

Ahh, the competition. Maija and Claire exchanged glances.

"Can I go now, Pop?" Johnny asked.

Big Jim nodded, and Johnny left. "*Maya,* like them ancient folks in the Yucatán?"

"Not quite. It's Finnish but pronounced the same."

"Right." He checked his watch. "Well, gotta supervise my dinner rush. If you need anything—a good margarita, the best food in town, some cooking tips, stop by."

"Thanks," she said, annoyed by the cooking tips comment. "We'll do that."

Baker turned to leave, then stopped. "I do have one piece of advice."

"What's that?"

"Some folks ain't happy that any ethnic restaurants are here. I had some trouble when I opened back in the nineties."

A spasm of tension hit her muscles. "Trouble?"

"Harassment, vandalism, crap like that. Watch your backs."

After Big Jim Baker left, Maija turned to Claire. "You think he's serious?"

Claire shrugged and scrunched her lips. "That was decades ago. Mexican cuisine's ubiquitous now. Shouldn't be a problem."

· · · · ·

As they packed up for the drive home that evening, Claire said, "Does it feel like we're at a slant?" She exaggerated a lean toward the backside of the truck.

Maija concentrated on her posture and balance. Sure enough, the rear left side of the truck felt noticeably lower. "Hmm. It seemed level when we arrived."

Claire stepped out and walked around the truck. After a moment, she said, "Gosh darn it. The tire's flat!"

Maija joined her, looked at the tire, and groaned.

"Should *we* try to change it?" Claire asked.

Neither of them had ever changed any sort of tire. That's what dads and AAA were for, right? Maija did a phone search and found a twenty-four-hour emergency service. The guy who answered said it'd be at least an hour before he arrived and a one-hundred-dollar minimum for the service call. Her spirits sank as she gave him their location.

Ninety minutes later, the repair truck arrived. The repairman changed the tire and pulled the culprit nail from the flat. "Because the puncture was so close to the sidewall," he said, "you'll have to buy a new tire."

"Are you sure?" Maija asked.

"As sure as I am that Norwegians love lutefisk," he said. "You risk your life if you drive on it with a patch job."

Maija paid him, then jammed the receipt into her pocket as the repairman drove away. "Great," she said. "This little mishap puts us even deeper in the red."

"It's only a minor setback," Claire said with a dismissive wave.

"Let's go." Maija trudged toward the driver's door. "We've lost enough sleep already."

• • • • •

On Saturday, Cocina Divina was parked adjacent to the Straight River soccer complex to work a youth tournament. Business was growing steadily. Maija's fish tacos were the surprise bestseller. During the final game of the tournament, customer traffic predictably dropped to zero. Everyone who wasn't playing was watching the championship game. Preoccupied with prepping for the anticipated post-game rush, Maija and Claire were startled by a horn honk.

In the parking lot, ten feet from their order counter, Big Jim Baker sat behind the wheel of a red pickup, his elbow on the rolled-down window. "Hey, *amigas*," he said, "did you know your truck has graffiti all over the backside?"

In unison, the partners dropped their jaws and said, "What?" then rushed outside to see for themselves. In large, neon-green letters across their banner and the siding, someone had spray-painted *Tacos From Hell* and *Mexican Food Sucks*.

"I can't believe it," Maija exclaimed as they returned to the order window. "How did we not notice?"

"Only takes a minute," Baker said. "The vandals wait until you're distracted. Splash-and-dash."

Claire said, "I suppose the police would laugh if we called. No witnesses, no suspects."

"Probably," Maija said. "Let's take that banner down. If we can't clean it tonight, we'll replace it ASAP."

· · · · ·

Two days later, Cocina Divina was working the light-industrial area of Straight River. Despite a persistent drizzle that dampened business, two other local restaurant owners stopped by to chat. Surprisingly, Johnny Baker returned, bought two fish tacos, and left immediately. But as two o'clock approached, the area was deserted.

"The restaurant owners in this town seem pretty supportive," Maija said during the lull, "even though we're taking away some of their customers."

"Competition is healthy," Claire said. "Your fantastic food will force them to get better. Then the entire town benefits."

"I guess. I just hope this rattletrap truck lets us compete for the rest of the summer."

"Hola, *chicas*." They both jumped as Big Jim's bulk filled their view out the order window. He cheerily asked, "Any other troubles lately?"

"Nope," Maija said.

Baker nodded. "Good to hear." Pointing past the rear of their truck, he said, "You oughta try those businesses someday. More workers there than you'd think."

Maija and Claire had just leaned out the order window to look when the quiet was broken by the sound of shattering glass. Maija's heart leaped into her throat. Claire shrieked. Baker flinched. They all turned toward the front of the truck.

"Oh my gosh!" Maija said.

Baker yelled, "Hey you, stop!" He lumbered around the corner of the building as fast as his beer belly allowed.

The women rushed to the truck's cab. Shards of windshield glass were strewn about. On the driver's seat lay a red brick.

"Holy cow," Claire said.

Maija slumped, fighting the urge to cry, then scream, then put her fist through another window.

Baker reappeared, panting. "Couldn't catch him, but I called the cops. Looked like some damned biker-skinhead neo-Nazi."

Panic chilled Maija's blood and showed on Claire's face. Maija squeaked out, "Neo-Nazi?"

Baker scowled. "Neo-Nazi, skinhead, white supremacist. Same diff. They hate anybody or anything that ain't white. A few years ago, some skinhead tossed a burning wooden cross into my dumpster. Luckily, someone called the fire department in time to prevent El Toro from going up in flames."

Fire? Maija's initial impulse was to close up and speed home. She looked at Claire as rain puddled in the driver seat. "Tape a trash bag over the hole. I'll call an auto glass repair truck."

A police officer showed up minutes later and took their statements. Folding her notebook, she said, "Don't hold your breath on this one, ladies. Could be one of a dozen people we've had trouble with before."

As Baker departed, he said, "You two be extra careful from now on . . . *if* you decide to come back."

Worry showed on Claire's face. "Something to consider, girlfriend, if only to cut down on the repair bills."

Unsaid was Claire's concern for their safety. Maija's heart and mind fought a pitched battle for dominance. *Stay vs. leave.* She stiffened with resolve and met Claire's eyes. "If we leave, they win. We're tougher than that. I'll only give up if no one buys my food."

· · · · ·

However, as she tallied the day's receipts at the kitchen table that night, Maija *did* consider switching to the Twin Cities market. One negative was fuel costs—a significant expense due to their truck's minimal gas mileage. A positive was the reduced likelihood of being hassled by skinheads in a big, crowded city. But it was hard to justify trading a solid customer base and growing sales for stiffer competition, increased permit costs, and longer driving distances.

Claire entered with a towel wrapped around her head, wearing a pink terrycloth robe and fuzzy slippers that looked like two Dalmatian puppies strapped to her feet.

Maija smiled and shook her head at her roommate's whimsical taste in footwear. The break in her concentration changed her thoughts back to the vandals. She said, "Aren't neo-Nazis into drugs, gang wars, overthrowing the government, big stuff like that?"

Claire stopped towel-drying her head and looked up through strands of wet hair. "I suppose."

"So why would they bother vandalizing a run-down little food truck in a small farm town?"

"Big Jim *said* it was a neo-Nazi. He was sure enough to call the police."

"But *we* never saw the culprit."

"True."

"Something doesn't add up," Maija said. "Most small towns are hostile toward newcomers, particularly minorities. Maybe some *closet* neo-Nazi who resents nonwhite anything, including ethnic restaurants, wants us gone. After all, El Toro has been the only Mexican restaurant here for decades. What if this closet neo-Nazi hired a *real* neo-Nazi to do their dirty work, figuring we'll be extra scared and leave sooner."

Claire furrowed her brow. "So how do we stop the vandalism?"

Maija contemplated the question. "Invite Zoie over. We need her tech expertise."

Claire placed the call, talked briefly, and clicked off. "She's on her way. What the heck are you thinking?"

Maija cracked a sinister smile. "Pour some wine, and I'll explain."

"Ooh, goody." Claire rubbed her hands together. "Wine and skullduggery. What fun."

· · · · ·

After getting Zoie's advice, Maija and Claire set their trap the next day. However, a week passed with no other incidents. Business continued to improve. Maija actually felt confident that Cocina Divina would become profitable. Maybe she was mistaken about suspecting a plot. Maybe the three incidents *were* coincidental lousy luck.

During a lull on the eighth day after the windshield incident, Big Jim strolled up, looking bemused. "Still here, huh?"

Maija nodded. "Despite the vandalism, business is too good to leave." She smiled. "Can we get you a fish taco?"

"Nope, just stopped on my way to El Toro." He did a slow

three-sixty as if noticing the lack of customers. "Gotta say I admire your courage. But I also want to say you're not the only vandalized restaurant in town. Someone threw a rock through my back window early this morning."

"Oh, dear," Maija said, shooting Claire a look of concern. Maybe real neo-Nazis *were* the culprits.

"I'm worried this vandalism spree is going to spread," Baker said. "I'll warn the Chinese and Indian places." He checked his watch. "Well, gotta go. Again, watch yourselves."

Maija said, "We'll try to grow eyes in the backs of our heads."

"Yeah. Good luck with that." Big Jim smiled wryly and walked to his truck.

Maija and Claire stepped outside and circled the truck, looking for signs of vandalism. After all, they'd missed the first three attacks, which all occurred in broad daylight. However, they found nothing suspicious and resumed working.

At 7:00, they closed and packed up. Maija slid behind the wheel, wondering if someone had pulled off some clandestine vandalism. *Dead battery? Engine fire? Exploding muffler?* After the motor turned over normally, she huffed out her held breath. "So far, so good."

Claire crossed her fingers. "Let's keep it that way."

They left the industrial park and drove homeward. As Maija braked before the turn onto the highway, the pedal felt spongier than usual. She pressed harder but barely made the turn on all four wheels.

Claire noticed the dangerous turn. "You been drinkin', girl?"

"Of course not. The darn brakes are wearing out faster than we anticipated."

"Better get 'em checked."

"I suppose," Maija said glumly. *Another profit-eating expense.*

Exhausted from the long day, they both fell silent. As they coasted to a stop at the signal light for their turnoff to home, Maija applied the brakes. The sponginess was worse. The truck rolled halfway into the intersection before it stopped.

Concern showed on Claire's face. "Take it easy the rest of the way."

Maija nodded. The light turned green, and she accelerated. The last few blocks to their apartment featured a long downhill toward a creek. When she applied the brakes, nothing happened.

"Brakes, Maija, brakes!" Claire said.

"I am!" Maija pressed harder. The truck didn't slow. Looking up, she panicked. "Oh my God!"

A couple pushing a baby stroller stepped into the street on the other side of the bridge. Maija stood on the brake pedal, but the truck still picked up speed. Claire inhaled a ragged gasp and pushed against her seatback. Maija honked the horn to warn the couple, who looked up and froze. Mere yards from a catastrophe, Maija swerved right and slammed head-on into the steel bridge railing. Glass smashed. Metal crunched and squealed. Both women were whipped forward, then backward against their headrests.

A seeming eternity passed as Maija digested what had happened. She'd almost killed three innocent strangers. She and Claire could've been seriously injured.

"You okay?" she asked Claire.

Trembling, Claire stammered, "I-I th-think so. You?"

Maija did a quick triage of her condition. "I'm okay."

They stepped out and approached the visibly shaken couple.

"What happened?" the woman asked.

"I am so sorry we scared you," Maija said. "The brakes failed." Sudden realization flashed into her brain. She grabbed Claire by the shoulders. "The vandals!"

Claire gasped. "Those scumbags!"

"Call the police," Maija said, stifling a primal scream. "I'll call a tow truck. Then we'll see about those lowlifes."

They spent the next hour dealing with the police and the wrecker. Maija warned the officer that they may have incriminating evidence against someone who tampered with the brakes. He gave her a business card and told her to call if she did.

After rushing home, Maija connected Zoie's video spy camera to her laptop. They'd mounted the device on the top left rear corner of the truck's blind side. They sped through the footage until they saw a young man with something in his hand creep up to the truck, crouch down, and roll underneath the front end. Moments later, he reappeared, stood, and faced the camera before slipping away. Perfectly captured on high-resolution video was Johnny Baker.

· · · · ·

When confronted by the Straight River Police, Johnny confessed to all the vandalism—including the flat tire—on the orders of Big Jim. Both men were arrested on misdemeanor charges. Genuinely remorseful, Big Jim hadn't dreamed that sabotaging the truck's brakes would cause an accident. He'd only told Johnny to put a pinhole puncture in the brake fluid line so Maija would notice and incur yet another repair expense. The Bakers' motivation was the desire to scare away the new competition—Cocina Divina. The neo-Nazi business was merely a ruse to divert suspicion. The Bakers pled guilty, paid a fine and restitution to Maija, and were placed on probation.

With the food truck a total loss, Maija found herself unemployed. She considered re-applying at her old firm, but the restaurateur bug had bitten hard. She ached to return to a kitchen. More than ever, she wanted to honor Abuela Sofia's wish.

As she browsed job-search websites for sous chef openings one afternoon, her phone rang. Caller ID indicated a Straight River prefix. Immediately suspicious, she answered.

It was Big Jim.

"You've got some nerve," Maija said, not masking her anger.

"Hold on a sec," he said. "I have a business proposition."

"A *what*?"

"I want to sell El Toro to you."

Maija almost dropped the phone. After regaining her composure, she said, "Is this another evil scheme you cooked up to harass me some more?"

"Nope. I'm a tired old man running a tired old restaurant." The weariness in his voice was palpable. "I shot my reputation in the foot with my . . . *misbehavior*. And I don't have the energy to turn things around. I want to retire. Johnny doesn't want to succeed me. Who better to take over than the Finnish-Mexican *chica* who makes killer fish tacos?"

"But I . . . I—"

"Please. Straight River needs a Mexican restaurant. We'll work out an affordable deal."

Maija's insides churned with anxiety and excitement. Was this golden opportunity *really* dropping into her lap?

"And, you can rename the place *Cocina Divina.*" This time, Big Jim pronounced the name with a polished, respectful Spanish accent.

FISH TACOS

Recipe courtesy of the de la Rosa family, Chill Aqui restaurant, Owatonna, Minnesota

Makes 8 tacos—4 servings

For the dredge:

2 cups self-rising flour

2 teaspoons baking powder

2 tablespoons granulated chicken bouillon (Knorr)

12 ounces Pacifico Clara beer

For the fish:

24 ounces Atlantic Cod filets, cut into 3-ounce portions

Coconut oil for deep frying

For the taco sauce:

4 tablespoons mayonnaise

2 cups ketchup

½ cup Valentina Sauce (Mexican hot sauce)

1 teaspoon mustard

For the garnish:

3 cups shredded green cabbage

½ cup shredded red cabbage

1 habanero pepper, sliced thin

2 teaspoons apple cider vinegar

½ teaspoon Mexican oregano

½ tablespoon granulated chicken bouillon (Knorr)

For the tacos:

8 6-inch diameter corn tortillas

Directions

1. Stir together dredge ingredients until smooth. Refrigerate for 10 minutes.

2. Combine taco sauce ingredients well. Let stand at room temperature.

3. Mix garnish ingredients and refrigerate.

4. Heat coconut oil to 350 degrees in a deep fryer or large pot so fish will not touch bottom or sides.

5. Dip individual pieces of cod into dredge, let excess drip off, and fry for 10 minutes or until batter is browned and crisp. Remove and drain.

6. Warm the tortillas on a hot griddle or frying pan for 30 seconds on each side.

7. Assemble tacos. Place one cod fillet on each warm tortilla. Top with garnish and drizzle with taco sauce. Serve immediately.

KISS AND TELL

By Diane Sismour

THE SWITCHBOARD LIGHTS up at the South Beach 9-1-1 call center. Gunshots fired at the Tottensville Marina are the only common denominator. Seven callers say they heard a different shot count. Nobody leaves a name and address to go along with the phone numbers logged except for one caller, Constance Fresca.

Driving down Main Street, Detective Colin Murphy spots another business that went belly-up and more houses bear foreclosure signs on the doors since his last trip to the marina. When he arrives at the scene, the parking area at 225 Ellis Street is empty except for two officers cordoning off the far end of the lot. Blue and red lights flood the docked fishing boats in the Tottensville Marina. A light rain falls, washing away evidence.

Exiting the unmarked Interceptor, he opens a golf umbrella and joins Sergeant Nelson and his rookie partner. An arctic wind has plummeted the hot, late July temperatures from the eighties into the fifties, making him feel every one of his sixty-two years. "I'm getting too old for this game." He flexes his fingers to loosen the joints.

"The South Shore hasn't had a homicide all year, Nelson. Thought your precinct got lucky," he says.

"Hoping it's the first and last." The sergeant turns away and calls in to dispatch. "The scene is contained, one victim, no witnesses. The EMTs came and left. Murphy's here. We're waiting on Wheeler."

"Rodger. CSU is in transit." He disconnects.

A gust of wind blasts them, and Murphy struggles to keep the giant parasol righted. Pointing out the footprints imbedded in the soft ground between the macadam and the house trailer, he says to the newbie, "Watch your step."

The rookie finishes taping the surround and double-checks the yellow caution-line. He hitches a thumb toward the door. "At least you can ID this guy. Your case in Annadale, didn't someone get rid of a federal witness in a furnace? It gives new meaning to ashes to ashes."

"Don't remind me. The Feds wanted the case. I said good riddance." Murphy studies the ground in front of the doorway. "Looks like our vic was popular." He squats to get closer. "Multiple flat heeled and high heel imprints. It'll take all night to cast these shoe prints."

Not wanting to add his size fourteens to the mix, he holds the umbrella over the footpath and waits behind the perimeter until the Crime Scene Unit arrives.

Ducking out of the zone, the rookie stands beside Murphy, and says, "Should be an open and shut."

"This better be open and shut. It's my last case."

"A few more years and I'll be right behind you, walking out that door," says Nelson. "I know this guy, Frank Fresca." He points to the other end of the parking lot. "He owns that restaurant—the best seafood in Staten Island."

"What else can you tell me?"

"Fresca's is a mob hangout, or it was. As far as I've heard, he wasn't part of the family. He looked the part, but you never know. The clientele followed his wife to Mother Anna's a few years ago when they split."

"Nothing is easy when it comes to murder, especially when the mob is involved. What else? There's always more."

The sergeant waggles his head and grins. "I heard he got beat up pretty good a few years ago—husband of another woman. That's when the wife left. This place will be a zoo soon when the press gets wind of the hit."

Murphy looks from Fresca's on the Bay, deserted at 12:25 on a Saturday night, to a block away. The lot at Mother Anna's Restaurant is full, and the place is lit up bright as a disco ball. Something is fishy about this case, and it isn't Today's Special.

Headlights flood the area as a crime scene team parks beside the cruiser. Within moments, a large pop-up tent is erected in front of the trailer. Halogen lights cast away shadows. A deeper high heel print, wider than the first, becomes noticeable. Cameras flash, capturing the details before the elements erode away clues as they wait for the medical examiner to arrive.

Murphy checks the house trailer. The door stands ajar just far enough for a muzzle to fit through. From this angle, the guy inside on the couch could be napping, but he knows a bullet-riddled corpse lies in there.

He waves a photographer over and points to the doorknob area. The camera flashes as another detective brushes dusting powder on the area revealing several finger swirls. Tape lifts the prints. Before opening the door, he listens for any movement. Although the rookie cleared the scene earlier, he calls out, "NYPD. Police."

Nelson moves in and takes the lead. "The last thing you want is to take a bullet just before retiring." He rechecks the single-unit trailer. Satisfied the assailant left, the sergeant returns to the doorway, "All clear."

"Thanks." Murphy enters and flits a penlight beam around the room. No muddy footprints, but scuffs disturbed the carpet and a thick layer of dust coats the furniture, all except the coffee table. If he had to guess, someone wiped it clean. He doubts they'll find any prints on light switches or doorknobs either. Nothing else appears touched near the body.

The white male victim, in his mid- to late-sixties, lounges on the couch slayed execution-style. Whoever shot Fresca killed him in anger or rage. Nine shots riddle the corpse—one to the forehead and eight to the body. Gray matter and blood splatter the walls and soak the white leather. Considering the victim has more holes than a Swiss cheese and pastrami on rye, Murphy expected to see more blood.

A wallet lies on the couch. He prods open the fold with the penlight, no cash, and a couple of credit cards. A driver's license identifies the deceased, Frank Fresca, sixty-six years old. He notes the address.

The crime scene team follows him inside, steering clear of the body. They dust the light switches, doorknobs, the faucets and countertop, anywhere someone might touch. Whoever wiped the prints cleaned up pretty well. No usable prints anywhere, not even from the victim.

Murphy moves to the kitchen, two cleaned forks and dinner plates rest in a plastic rack. No drips, the bottom tray holds water. The trash contains a foil take-out container and two empty wine bottles. One empty wineglass sits on the counter, another glass has been knocked to the floor. Red wine splatters have soaked into the white leather couch and into the carpet. Red lipstick rims one of the glasses. "He had company."

He follows the narrow hallway to the bedroom at the opposite end of the trailer. The closet door is open, and inside is an old safe taking up half the floor space. "The thing must weigh two hundred and fifty pounds. Nobody could snatch and run with that monster."

The safe is wide open. The top shelf holds some record books with an empty space beside them, and ammunition for a .22 caliber weapon. On the bottom shelf, the dust along the outside edge suggests someone removed whatever was inside. "Add robbery to the case."

Headlights flash through the bedroom window from the lot. He caught a good night. The M.E. arrived in record time. He returns to the victim.

Medical Examiner Dana Wheeler walks into the trailer and the oxygen in the room sucks out. All energy and brains packed into a knockout body. She carries the heavy equipment cases into the room as if they're shopping bags from a sale at Bloomingdale's and assesses the scene. "Good to see you, Murphy. I heard you're retiring after this one."

"News travels fast. I entered the force in '79. It's been a long run."

She gives him a rare gift—her full attention and a smile. "A shame. Such talent sent out to pasture."

"You sound as though you're going to miss me."

She looks toward the body and tilts her head. "You picked a doozy for a last case." She uses a laser pen to point at the wounds. "Those look like they're done by a pro, though scattered. A small caliber gun, from the holes in him."

"There's ammo for a .22 in the bedroom."

"I'll confirm that as soon as we can get the body to the morgue."

She calls out to the team, "We're going to be here for a while, boys and girls. Get bullet trajectories and blood splatter tests."

While opening one of the metal cases, she calls over her shoulder, "I'll keep you in the loop, Murphy."

· · · · ·

The next morning, Murphy lets his witnesses sweat in the interrogation rooms while he observes them through the two-way mirrors. Room One holds an employee from Fresca's. Terry Angeloni, married, has lived on the same street since he was born, no priors. His day-old beard doesn't fit his clean preppy image. He thumps the metal table with his thumbs like a drum set. He's either nervous as hell or high.

In Room Two, a woman sits on the metal chair with hands on the table and eyes closed. A clip ties back her graying hair, and she wears no makeup. Splotches from this morning's prep work stain her white coat. Embroidered above the chest pocket is *Constance Fresca, Executive Chef, Mother Anna's Restaurant.*

He carries in a tissue box and drops it on the table in front of Constance Fresca, startling the witness awake.

"I'm Detective Colin Murphy. My condolences, Mrs. Fresca."

The sudden arrival, and remorseful greeting, brings an emotion he didn't expect from the estranged wife. The tears seeping aren't onion tears. Unashamed, she lets them run.

"Call me Connie." She sits taller in the chair and swipes the tears away.

He takes a seat across from her. "Tissue?"

"No, thanks." She rubs her cheeks dry. "Frank was an idiot, but he didn't deserve to die like that."

"Mrs. Fresca . . ."

She interrupts. "Connie."

"Connie, where were you between 9:30 and 12:30 last night?"

"In the kitchen until the meal tickets stopped around 10:00. I made dinner for Frank and me. Met him at the trailer beside Fresca's. The one his mama lived in. He said he wanted to talk. He broke up with his girlfriend and couldn't get her and her brats out of my house."

"Her name?"

"Veronica Constanelli."

Murphy notes the information. If Fresca wanted the girlfriend to leave, he wouldn't have kept it a secret.

"How long were you separated?"

She didn't pause to think about the answer. "Thanksgiving will be four years."

"Why did you meet with him?"

"He hadn't signed the divorce papers. I wanted them signed one way or another. He is . . . *was* a sucker for my cooking."

"Did you just say you threatened the victim to sign the divorce papers? I have to ask—did you kill your husband?"

"No. The divorce would give me back Fresca's Restaurant and my house on Girard Street. He wouldn't have to give me any support payments. He'd get to keep the marina, the sales office, and the two trailers. I was getting what I wanted . . . killing him would give me his debt. He never did manage money well. I can't imagine how bad things got since I left."

"Why did you separate?"

She shrugs and looks away.

He asks again, "Why did you separate?"

"After cheating on me three and a half years ago, his girlfriend's soon-to-be-ex must have found out. Four guys came into the restaurant with guns, and he got beat up. It's in the records somewhere, I'm sure. He landed in the hospital with broken ribs and fingers. His head needed twelve stitches. I wanted no part in his life after that."

· · · · ·

She remembers last night in detail, not that she'd tell the cop anything. She knew Frank would watch the surveillance monitors and waited motionless to avoid the cameras catching movement. He finally left the restaurant and drove his car across the lot to the house trailer. When he inserted the key into the trailer door lock, she headed for him and her shoe hit gravel.

He froze.

Shit, he heard me. "If Louie the Hammer waited for you, you'd be dead before the caliber collapsed in the lock," she said.

"You know me better than anyone. Shut down the kitchen, then check on Mama. Since Mama went to a home, I have a little wine in quiet before going home. The bitch never shuts her yap. No wonder Louie sent her packing."

Connie brought the revolver to within inches of his ear. Killing him then wouldn't give her the satisfaction of seeing his face when he signed the restaurant over to her. The snap of metal slamming metal clipping close behind him forced a gasp. "That was the first empty chamber. The safety round, just like you taught me, Frankie. The rest are loaded."

He turned to face her. His gaze focused to stare down the unwavering barrel of her snub-nose Smith and Wesson revolver. She had the short muzzle aimed square between his eyes.

"You never should have taught me how to shoot," she said. He slid a step left. She moved the pistol to follow with dead on accuracy. "I've been practicing too."

"Pick a head, Frankie? The one you think with or the one you fuck with . . . one of them is getting capped if you don't sign the damned divorce papers." Her hands tightened around the grip of the gun before shifting the weapon lower.

"You're serious this time," he said.

"Give me a reason to shoot. You know I will."

"Did you bring it?"

She removed one hand from the weapon and fished through her purse for the paperwork without taking her eyes off him. A sealed envelope with RETURN TO SENDER scrawled across the front, and a bright, red, lipstick kiss. "Nice touch. Tell Ms. Constanelli I know where to find her if she interferes again."

"Dinner. Did you bring dinner?" He tilted his head back and looked to the heavens for help. "If I don't eat soon, someone's head is going to roll."

"I'm not one of your line cooks. They're the ones afraid of you, idiot. Not me."

"They better be or they'd be working at Mother Anna's."

"Hate to break this to you, but my tables were full tonight."

· · · · ·

Murphy asks, "What did you cook?" breaking her from her thoughts.

"When I was the chef at Fresca's, mussels in white wine and tomato sauce with fresh linguine was one of my specials. His favorite meal."

"His last meal."

"We shared a bottle of *his* wine. He signed the papers, and I cleaned the coffee table and dishes. He was fine when I left at about 10:30. After returning to the restaurant and looking over the paperwork, I realized he missed a signature. I walked back to the trailer and found him shot dead."

"You had one bottle of wine, not two?"

Her face flushes, and the vein in her forehead protrudes and pulses. She closes her eyes, and her jaw tightens. After taking several deep breaths, the woman rubs her temples and then opens her eyes. She still appears in pain, but she also has focus. Something here made sense only to her.

"If he had a second bottle, it wasn't with me."

"Why did you leave the scene?" he asks.

"I called 9-1-1 and left in case whoever killed him was still around."

The realization that she just turned from a witness to a suspect registers. She gasps and slaps the table as she speaks. "Wait a damned minute . . . I gave my name, number, and address to the operator. I don't have time for this. In case you don't realize, I'm a busy woman, and the lunch preps still need to get done. Unless you're charging me with murder, I have to get back to work." Both hands slam the table. "I didn't kill my husband. He was worth more to me alive than dead."

He'll have to dig up more on Connie Fresca.

"Don't leave town, Mrs. Fresca." He presses the intercom button. "Mrs. Fresca is free to go."

• • • • •

In Room Two, Terry Angeloni sits in the bolted-down metal chair. Gel slicks his hair back, and his clothes look fresh off the rack. So fresh, he missed a tag.

Armed with photos of the victim, Murphy enters. The kid goes from drumming the table to bouncing his leg. "I'm Detective Colin Murphy, my condolences for your boss."

The kid acts confused and stops mid-bounce. "What do you mean . . . Frank is dead?"

Murphy doesn't answer. He moves to stand behind the witness. "Tell me about your boss, Frank Fresca."

"He was okay. You know, a boss."

"No, I don't know, Terry. That's why I'm asking you."

The kid doesn't answer right away. "He was picky. If something was out of place, instead of doing it himself, he'd call me over and make me fix it. He could have moved the damned vase himself."

Murphy walks around the table to face him and places a manila envelope between them. He leans toward the witness with his hands flat on the top. At six feet five inches tall, he's learned how to use his size to intimidate a punk. "Word on the street says he was a prick to work for, not some lazy asshole."

Angeloni sinks back into the chair. His hands gesticulate with each phrase. "You have no idea. He'd fire someone for nothing. You did things his way, or you were out." Both of his legs are bouncing now. "Vendors are looking for him, hunting him down. I'm back two months on the rent. He hasn't paid us since the middle of June. I'm getting eviction notices."

The detective stays quiet. The seconds drag out.

"Things got bad. The regulars stopped coming. The place was tanking fast." The kid sits still. "I heard the Feds showed up yesterday and took over the docks, turning boats away."

Murphy's radar spots some truth to his story—the Feds again. He sits across from him and waits.

"I got a call not to come in to work yesterday. He owed me three-large.

To hell with him, I went and found another job. When I came to get my stuff, the lights were out. Saturday night, this place should've been hopping busy."

"What time were you at the restaurant?"

"Just after 11:00. Pop never misses the evening news. I had to leave. All that shit about the government bailing out the banks—what about me? Who's going to bail me out?"

"If you end up in the slammer, we'll see."

Angeloni freezes. If looks could kill, Murphy would be dead.

"That's not what I meant, and you know it. I left when the news started. Like I said, no customers, no lights, empty. The boss was in the trailer across the lot. Everyone knows not to bother him there."

The detective stands and circles behind him again. He paces back and forth, before returning to the table to stare eye-to-eye across from the witness. Pounding a fist on the table, he asks, "Did you go in the trailer last night?"

The kid wipes his palms on his jeans. His breathing comes in short puffs. "No," he says, his eyes cast down.

"We took shoe molds of all the imprints leading to the trailer. Are you sure you weren't there last night? We're going to find out." He looks under the table and takes a stab at his shoe size. His sneakers have some muddy residue along the edges. "Terry, my guess, you're a size ten in those Adidas? It's best to say something now."

Murphy punches the intercom button. "I need two evidence bags."

Angeloni can't sit still. Both his knees bounce. "I wanted to get paid," he blurts.

"Remove your shoes."

The door opens, and the rookie from last night enters. "Hey, how's it going?"

"Take those shoes to evidence. Have them processed."

He nods to Murphy, bags the shoes, and exits.

"How am I supposed to walk home?" cries Angeloni.

"You're not going anywhere for a while."

Murphy opens the envelope and slaps three photos onto the table one at a time. "What happened? He didn't pay you so you shot him?"

The kid's face blanches as the sight of the third image. "He was out cold on the couch. An empty wine bottle was in front of him, his glass dumped. I thought he passed out drunk. His wallet laid open on the couch. I just took the cash. I didn't kill him. I swear."

"Where was the wine bottle?"

"On the table. What's that got to do with anything?"

"I'm asking the questions here. Did you see anyone else in or near the trailer?"

"No. Not that I saw."

"Are you positive? You just said you didn't go into the trailer, now you did. Think hard. Was anyone else there?"

Angeloni clutches the table edge. Through clenched teeth, he says, "No."

Murphy can smell Angeloni sweating—fear. He collects the photos and leaves.

· · · · ·

A leggy thirtysomething woman with long blonde hair enters the South Shore's 123rd Precinct. She looks poured into a tight, black sweater and pleather leggings. All eyes turn toward her as she totters on narrow heels to the front desk. Her purse matches her lips—bright, red, and shiny.

"I'm Veronica Constanelli. Someone here wants to talk to me about my Frankie." As if on cue, a tear slides down her cheek and she sniffs.

The receptionist points to vinyl-covered chairs lined along the wall. "Have a seat. Someone will be with you in a moment." She slides a tissue box across the counter toward Constanelli and waves for the attention of the next walk-in. The hum of business as usual returns.

Watching the show from the monitor in the detectives office, Murphy studies Veronica Constanelli as she looks from the receptionist, to the chairs, and back again. Her quivering lip has no effect on the woman.

Constanelli snatches two tissues from the box and walks over to the sitting area. Fidgeting on the worn vinyl, she poses as the distraught widow when she thinks anyone is watching, dabbing at her eyes and flapping the tissues to help dry the mascara. When nobody takes any interest, she removes a small mirror, applies lip gloss, and makes duck-lip pouts.

She's playing teenager at thirty years old, thought Murphy. This department has no time for someone who needs babysitting.

An officer escorts Veronica Constanelli into Room One. Murphy watches her through the mirror. The woman is no stranger to the inside of a jail cell. Her rap sheet lists charges for shoplifting, assault, and a DUI. Divorced from Louie Capelini, a.k.a. Louie the Hammer, she is the daughter of Martin Lazaro (deceased), a jeweler in Annadale, New York.

A familiar name—the FBI took over the Lazaro murder case from the start. Turned out, the jeweler laundered the mob's money in exchange for protection. They left out the part about protecting him from themselves when he turned evidence against the Family.

When he walks into the interrogation room, Constanelli cries, "Does no one care that my boyfriend is in the morgue?"

Her high, nasal voice pushes Murphy's patience tolerance button. "I'm Detective Colin Murphy. Ms. Constanelli, I'm sorry for your loss, but I have some questions for you as well. Where were you between 9:30 and 12:30 last night?"

"Frankie hadn't been home in three days. Some nights he sleeps in the trailer after a busy day. But three days in a row . . . something was going on. I went to the restaurant, and the place was closed."

He waits. Silence stretches.

"No cars, except his was in the lot. I was about to go into the trailer, when I heard her."

"Who?"

"That bitch, Connie. They were talking about 'old times,'" she mocks, her fingers emphasizing as quotes. "I looked through the window. She made him dinner *and* they had wine."

Constanelli turns away, and this time, the perfect makeup she applied this morning goes to hell. Mascara streaks her face, and her eyes puff worse than his swell after a tequila weekend binge. He hands her the tissue box.

"You saw Connie and Frank having dinner. What did you do?"

"Hid around the corner until she left, then I shoved the door open before he locked it. I'll never forget the look on his face. He turned white when he saw me. He asked what I was doing there. I pushed him inside. He insisted they were just signing the divorce papers. The ones I sent back."

• • • • •

She remembers him complimenting her on how she handled returning the paperwork. "Nice touch with the lipstick kiss-off." He had smiled and selected a bottle of wine from the kitchen cabinet.

• • • • •

Murphy asks, "Why did you mail back the divorce papers?"

"Because she wanted the house back," she says, with an eye roll. "I wasn't about to live in that trailer with two kids. He actually asked what was wrong, said that the trailer was good enough for Mama. Have you seen the place? It's a dump."

"Yes, ma'am. What happened next?"

"He was kidding, thank God, and wanted to celebrate. That's when Frankie told me about the place in the Caymans, a house the bitch didn't know about. We were leaving on Monday. I told him I'd need new clothes . . . and a bathing suit. He emptied his wallet. I told him I needed more."

When Murphy raises his brows, she says, "It's the tropics. I needed a whole wardrobe. I tapped my foot so he knew I wasn't leaving without more cash."

"How much money did he give you?"

"I snagged the bills before he started counting and shoved them into my coat pocket. Frankie said to stay in the living room. He walked into the bedroom and closed the door. I remember applying more lipstick. The package said the serum would plump lips better than injections."

She looks toward the two-way mirror and puckers. "What do you think?"

"I'm not at liberty to say."

"Anyway, I asked him if he wanted more wine and filled his glass, because he always wants more wine. I drank the rest from the bottle, just a few sips. You know, bottoms up. He wanted to sit on the couch, but I knew where he was going. I told him, I don't have time for no hanky-panky. I had to pack the kids' suitcases."

"Where are your children now?"

"The kids are with Louie's mom. I dropped them off early this morning. Then I heard about Frankie on the television. You think somebody would have told me."

Her hands shake, and her breath hiccups. Murphy can tell she's on the edge of another meltdown. "How much more money did he give you?"

"He handed me a stack of hundreds. Frankie really did love me. I thanked him with a big smooch and left. I did nothing wrong. He was alive when I left him. Why would I want him dead? We were leaving for the Cayman Islands in two days."

"Word has it he wanted you out of the house. Was this his way to get your bags packed? Maybe you figured it out and shot him?"

The shrill hits another octave when she screams, "That bitch. She's the one who wants me out. Frankie loved me."

· · · · ·

Murphy's cubical is one of four in the office. Each shift uses the same desks. His drawers, and in and out baskets, hold nary any paperwork by comparison. After several hours, a folder on each interview thickens with facts and fiction.

A knock sounds from the door. The person doesn't wait for an answer and walks in.

Dana Wheeler stands before him, folder in hand, and points at the "Retired" mug collecting pens on the desk. "Nice touch."

"Only one more month." He leans back in the chair. "An early going-away gift from the guys. What have you got for me?"

"Nothing as fancy as your mug. Here is the coroner's report on your vic, Frank Fresca." She hands him the file. "You just got a twist in the case."

"Even better." This close, he can smell her shampoo—sour apple. He takes time to read the report, watching her above the page. He is going to miss this view.

"Thanks for the evidence. It's time to give my condolences to Fresca's mother."

· · · · ·

On August second, summer temperatures and humidity return, and so do the tourists. Murphy cranks the air conditioning on the drive to the Sunrise Nursing Home. The Staten Island Expressway has more cars standing still than the mall parking garage at Christmas. At the nursing home, he finds a space near the entrance.

Staying here must cost a bundle, from the paved garden paths to the building's fancy brick architecture.

An attendant meets him at the entrance and walks with him to the room of Gianna Fresca. "She has her good days and bad. You're in luck," she says.

The door to the room is open, and indirect sunlight beams in through the window. The apartment's walls and furnishings are in soft beige and gold hues. Gianna Fresca sits in a recliner watching birds perched on a close branch. Calming music plays.

She squints at us when I knock on the door.

"Frankie, is that you?" she asks. The woman fumbles to place her glasses on, but tangles the cord looped over her neck.

"I'm Detective Colin Murphy. Let me help you, ma'am." He fits the spectacles on the bridge of her nose and steps back. I'm here to—"

"Are you here to play with Frankie? He's outside. Do you want a cookie?"

"No, ma'am. I'd like to—"

"The cookies are in the jar on the counter. Take all you'd like. Frankie won't eat them."

Murphy kneels on one knee beside the woman's chair. "Why can't Frankie eat the cookies?"

She worries her hands. "Frankie won't eat cookies." She looks out the window. "Are you here to play with Frankie? He's outside."

He adjusts the blanket covering her lap. "Mrs. Fresca, I'm sorry to bear this news, but Frankie died two days ago. My condolences."

The woman's small, wrinkled hand covers his. "Frankie is a good boy. Are you here to play with Frankie?"

"Yes, ma'am. I'll look for him outside."

Although she's smiling, her eyes mist and her face creases in worry. The person trapped inside her mind must know why he came here today—and it wasn't to play with Frankie.

· · · · ·

On the return trip, Murphy calls Wheeler. "Fresca's mother has dementia, but he might be allergic to something in cookies. What is in a cookie that could have killed him?"

"Nut or spice allergies can cause anaphylactic shock. A heart condition, high blood pressure, even a high-stress situation during the height of the allergic reaction could give him a heart attack."

"Thanks, kiddo. I owe you one." He grins knowing he owes her for a ton of favors.

"How about beers at the Southside Bar Friday night?" she asks.

"I owe you more than a beer. How about dinner?"

"Hold up, cowboy. After you retire, we'll talk restaurants."

"Deal." Here he thought life after the daily grind would be boring. "That's when this case wraps or the end of August."

"Think of our date as an added incentive," she says. He can hear her laughing as she disconnects.

The added incentive has him calling dispatch. "Have a cruiser pick up three suspects for questioning in Frank Fresca's murder. You can find Mrs. Connie Fresca at Mother Anna's Restaurant, Veronica Constanelli at the victim's home address on Girard Street, and Terry Angeloni at his apartment on Arthur Kill Road. If missing, put a BOLO out on them."

Earlier, he had done some digging on the widow. The niece of Marty the Rod, held by the FBI in the incineration of their witness, saw more than a few funeral corpses growing up. In the 1960s and 1970s, the mob held all the rackets—drugs, gambling, prostitution. They respected no law, but their own.

By the time he returns from the nursing home, Connie Fresca is sitting in the same interrogation room as her previous precinct visit. Her wrists are cuffed and shackled to the tabletop. She resisted arrest.

He takes the folder off his desk and observes her. "This should be fun," he mutters, before entering Interrogation Room One.

"What's so important that you have me brought in right before the dinner rush?"

"Your husband died from anaphylaxis shock from an allergic reaction, Mrs. Fresca, and you cooked him his last meal. Did you poison your husband?"

"What?"

Her reaction from furious to inquisitive appears genuine. He slaps photographs of the deceased on the table one at a time—the crime scene, a head shot, and, lastly, a shot of her husband sewn together in the morgue. Puckered skin marks the bullet wounds.

"Connie Fresca, did you give your husband a fatal dose of a known allergen?"

The pictures of her husband don't upset her. "An allergic reaction? No. As I said the other day, that was his favorite meal. He ate it all the time."

"What was your husband allergic to, Mrs. Fresca?"

"Cinnamon. He wouldn't let anything with cinnamon in the restaurant. Any desserts had to have all the recipes call for nutmeg instead. We didn't have any dessert that night. There's no call for those spices in my recipe."

There's a knock at the door and Murphy answers the interruption. "Uncuff her."

Murphy waits to continue questioning her until the officer removes the cuffs and leaves. "Did your husband own a house in the Cayman Islands?

"Not that I'm aware," she replies.

"Did you know about the safe in the house where you met your husband the night he was killed?"

"Yes. The money is Gianna's. The cash came from selling her house to pay for the nursing home. Her dementia worsened, and she couldn't take care of herself anymore. Frankie moved her into the trailer until he found a place he liked. He didn't trust the nursing home and wanted to pay monthly."

She places her head in her hands, then jolts up and says, "Oh my God, tell me the money is still there."

"For an estranged couple, you know a lot about your husband's everyday business."

"I've known Gianna since Frankie and I were kids. He was never good with money. She made me her legal guardian. He had to tell me about the safe in case something happened to him."

"Do you know the combination?"

"Yes. The combination is Gianna's birthday."

"What else was in the safe?"

Connie hesitates. "It doesn't hurt to spill it now. She can't remember anymore. His mama ran numbers after her husband died. She kept notes. She said they were her security."

"What other security did she have? There was ammunition for a .22 caliber weapon. Ballistics show someone used the gun in a homicide in April. Gianna Fresca doesn't appear capable of gunning down a man in an alley four months ago."

The suspect clams up and shakes her head.

Everything she said rings true with him or is easy enough to check. "I'm letting you go. Again, don't leave town."

· · · · ·

Before entering Interrogation Room Two, he says to a patrol officer, "Drive Mrs. Fresca back to the restaurant."

He reads the newest results from the swabs taken of the wineglass at the scene.

Through the mirror, he watches Veronica Constanelli pace around the room. She wears jeans, a tight tank top, and no makeup with her hair piled high on her head. Her lips don't seem as puffy.

He enters the room, "Please, sit."

"What's this all about? I told you everything I know."

"The active ingredient in the lipstick you wore the night Frank Fresca was murdered is cinnamon."

"And?"

"Frank Fresca died of anaphylaxis shock from an allergic reaction."

"I saw the pictures. He was *shot* dead."

"Did you know Frank Fresca was allergic to cinnamon?"

"Cinnamon? No. That explains why he never ordered dessert. What's him being allergic to cinnamon have to do with me?"

"You stated that you kissed him after he gave you ten thousand dollars then you left."

"Yes, so . . ."

"Your lipstick kiss killed Frank Fresca. Veronica Constanelli, you're under arrest for involuntary manslaughter in the death of Frank Fresca."

· · · · ·

Terry Angeloni jolts when Murphy walks into Interrogation Room One. There are black smudges beneath his eyes, and he's twitchy. He wears the same clothes from two days ago and stinks. The chains shackling his wrists to the table jangle.

"I heard you were about to run. Let me tell you how this is going to play out, Terry. The gun used to shoot Frank Fresca was used in another murder four months ago. Are you ready to go to jail for life?"

The kid grabs for the table edge and his eyes roll back, as he slides down the chair. He dangles from the cuffs. Murphy presses the help button beside the intercom.

They uncuff the kid, lean him against the wall, and snap open an ammonia capsule. He comes around real quick, gagging.

"Let's get you some water, and we'll try this again." They set Angeloni back on the chair and snap the cuffs round his wrists. Murphy returns to the room with a water bottle.

"Okay, kid. Breathe and answer me. Terry Angeloni, did you kill Dominic Lazaro in the alley behind his jewelry store on the night of April 22, 2008?"

"No. I don't even know the guy."

"Did you shoot Frank Fresca on the night of July 30, 2008?"

No answer. The words seem stuck in his throat.

"Let me refresh your memory," says Murphy. "You went to the trailer last Saturday night to get paid money owed you. You went into the trailer and what happened?"

"His girlfriend just left. I waited for her to walk away. The door was open. I didn't kill him. He was flailing around on the couch when I got there. His wine went everywhere. He kept saying to get his pen and pointing down the hall. I told him, I'm done taking orders from him. He started gagging. I went down the hall. Didn't see no pen. The safe door was open. Inside was a duffle bag filled with cash." He sips more water and stares at the surveillance camera above the door.

"What happened next? Terry, do you want to go to jail for the rest of your life?"

The words, *you* and *jail*, snap him to the present. "What the fuck, he owed everyone thousands. Here he had a stash. The gun you're talking about was inside the safe. It wasn't mine."

"How did he get full of lead? You had the gun—he owed you money—your family was being evicted—you killed him. It takes real rage to stare someone in the eye and shoot them nine time."

"He was dead. I swear. When I returned to the living room, he wasn't breathing. He just laid there. I checked his pulse. I wanted to yell at him for my family, for all of us he owed money. He could have paid us. Before I knew it, my finger was pulling back on the trigger, until there were no more bullets. I ran."

"Where did you stash the money and the gun?"

I threw the gun into the water off the dock where the Feds were searching the other day. Figured they wouldn't be looking there again."

Smart kid. "Where's the money"

"I gave the other waiters and cooks what he owed them, paid the rent, and bought some clothes. The rest is in my closet on the top shelf."

Murphy slides a pad of paper and a pen across the desk. "Write everything down. If you confess everything you told me, including where the money is from the safe, we can help you. If you don't, kiss your life good-bye."

When the detective leaves the room, he finds the assistant chief watching through the two-way mirror. "You have yourself a modern-day Robin Hood. Don't let the press get wind of that or the public will demand leniency."

· · · · ·

Tourists left after Labor Day. Fresca's on the Bay is closed permanently. Connie Fresca changes the sign, gathers the old staff, and opens Mama's Restaurant. Their soft opening is reserved for a party of two.

The warm fall breeze washes the heat off the shore. Colin Murphy and Dana Wheeler dine at an outside table overlooking the docks watching the sunset across the bay. The lantern light softens her stress lines formed from all the cases worked on the force.

He can't imagine how she sees him or why she'd want to date him. Right now in this moment, he doesn't care. He has a beautiful woman sitting across from him, and the sky has more colors than a Monet sunset.

"You pulled in all your favors, Murphy. The judge moved the case forward on the docket. You can officially retire."

"I wanted this case behind me. Too many people didn't deserve for their lives to be kept on hold." He remembers Gianna Fresca at her son's funeral. The procession to pay respects went out the funeral home door and around the block. She didn't remember them, but they haven't forgotten her. The community pitched in to support her care until a trust is established after probate.

"That kid got lucky," she says. "The press had his back as Robin Hood of South Shore."

"Six months for desecrating a corpse." He laughs. "I had him thinking he was going away for life."

"I think the judge couldn't deal with the grieving girlfriend's constant crying on the stand. She got off with community service."

Murphy watches the sun fade below the horizon. "She didn't know about his allergy. Otherwise, she'd have been nailed with serving twelve months for involuntary manslaughter. With good behavior, she'd have gotten out in six."

Connie delivers oysters on the half shell, champagne, and three glasses to the table. After pouring the champagne, she raises a glass and toasts, "To finding the truth surrounding Frank's death."

Murphy raises his, "To the good guys winning."

STEAMED MUSSELS IN WHITE WINE AND TOMATO SAUCE

Recipe courtesy of Mother Anna's Restaurant in the North End, Boston, Massachusetts. Source: https://www.thecomfortofcooking. com/2011/02/steamed-mussels-in-white-wine-and-tomato-sauce. html. Mussels and tomato sauce adapted from Epicurious.

Yield: Serves 2–3

Ingredients for tomato sauce

3 tablespoons extra-virgin olive oil

1 medium onion, finely chopped

2 garlic cloves, finely chopped

1 (28- to 32-ounce) can whole tomatoes in juice

1 teaspoon salt, or to taste

1 teaspoon sugar (optional), or to taste

Ingredients for mussels

1½ tablespoons extra virgin olive oil

2 garlic cloves, minced

¼ teaspoon dried hot red pepper flakes

½ cup dry white wine

2 cups tomato sauce (recipe included)

2 pounds mussels, scrubbed

Directions for tomato sauce

Preheat oven to 325 degrees F.

In a large saucepan, heat oil over medium low. Add onions and garlic, cooking and stirring until softened, about 5 minutes.

Add tomatoes, including juice, and salt. Cover and put in oven for 1½–2 hours, stirring and mashing tomatoes with a fork occasionally, until sauce is thickened and reduced to about 3 cups. If sauce tastes too acidic, add sugar and cook 5 minutes more.

Directions for mussels

In a large, heavy pot (I use a 5.5 quart Le Creuset), heat oil over medium low. Add garlic and red pepper flakes, cooking and stirring for 2 minutes. Increase heat to medium high. Add wine and bring to a boil. Add tomato sauce and mussels and cook over moderately high heat, covered, stirring occasionally, until mussels just open wide, 6 to 8 minutes. Discard any mussels that are unopened after 8 minutes. Serve immediately.

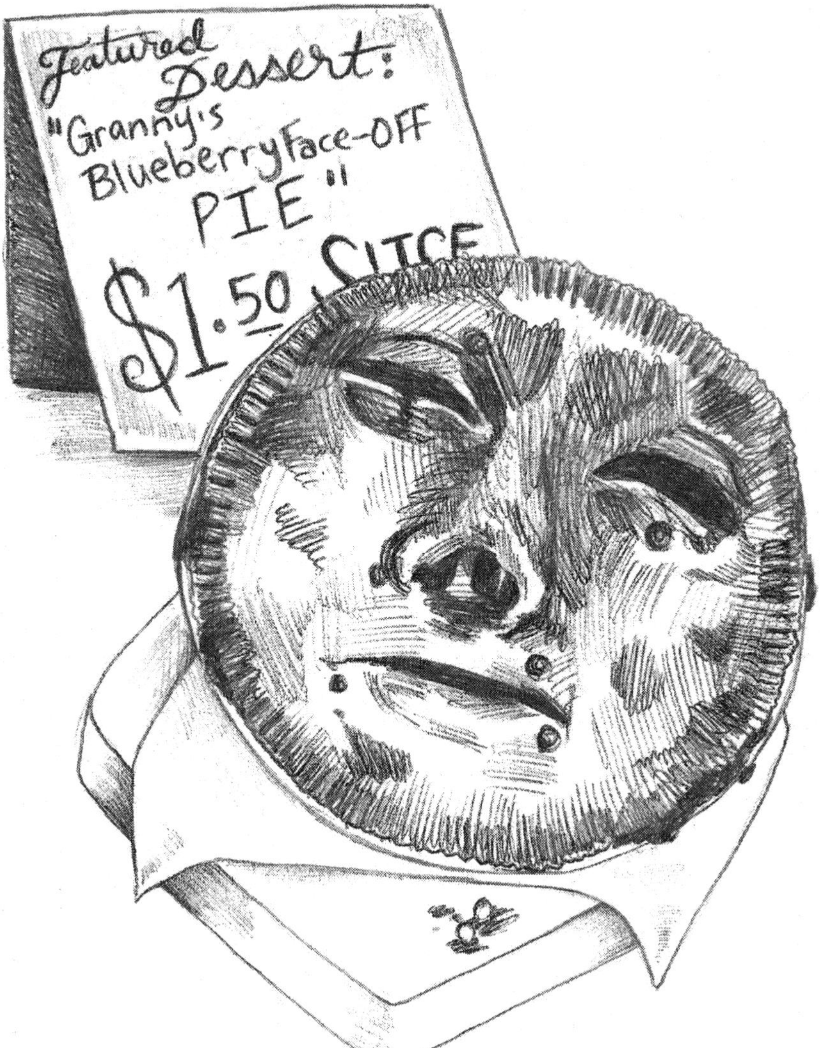
Featured Dessert:
"Granny's Blueberry Face-OFF PIE"
$1.50

OUT OF WHACK EVENT

By David Housewright

THE MYSTERY AUTHOR and the theater critic were late to the jazz club. The play the critic had been asked to review went well past its advertised length, so by the time they descended the long staircase to the basement—the best jazz joints are always in the basement—all of the tables were occupied. They managed to muscle themselves a spot at the crowded bar, yet before they could order, the critic spotted an unoccupied table directly behind a thick pillar that she assumed was meant to hold the building upright. Beggars not being choosers, the couple took possession of the table. From where she sat, the critic could see half of the stage; the author less than that and only if he leaned in a manner that practically put him in the critic's lap, a not altogether unpleasant experience he told her.

The Eastside Jacks were holding court from the stage. *New Orleans Traditional Jazz Quarterly* declared they were "a true authentic New Orleans dance hall-style band," and the author certainly wouldn't argue with that, listening intently as the six musicians began playing "Palm Court Strut." It took him a moment before he realized that the waiter had materialized next to the table to take the couple's drink orders. The critic requested a Riesling because she liked sweet wines. He ordered bourbon on the rocks because, dammit, they were listening to traditional jazz in a basement.

One and a half songs later, the waiter reappeared with the drinks. That's when the author felt a hand on his shoulder. He spun in his chair.

He noticed her legs before he noticed her; they were nice legs, yet time and experience had taught him not to stare. Looking up, he found a pale face, blue eyes, and blonde hair, a true Minnesota girl. She spoke before he did.

"This is my table," she said.

The waiter responded before the author could. Gesturing at a newly vacant table an arm's length away, he said "You could sit here."

The woman's face grew determined.

"This is my table," she repeated.

The theater critic was quick to notice the improvement in geography.

"Fine with us," she said.

She and the author took their beverages and moved to the empty table, which had an unobstructed view of the stage. The woman took up residence at the first table, sitting directly behind the pillar; even with some Olympic-quality gymnastics, she couldn't see around it.

She smiled, nodded at the couple, and said, "Thank you." The critic smiled and nodded back. The waiter was pleased that a potentially awkward scene had been defused and quietly retired. The author stared.

The mystery author taught the occasional novel-writing course at the Loft Literary Center in Minneapolis and encouraged his students to be always on the lookout for what his pal Libby Fischer Hellmann called "the out-of-whack event." A young woman insisting on sitting behind a pillar would certainly seem to qualify.

He turned toward the critic.

"Why would she do that?" the author asked.

"Shhh."

The critic gestured toward the stage as the Jacks started performing "Muskrat Ramble." She knew how the author's mind worked and refused to encourage him for fear he would spend the rest of the evening regaling her with fanciful scenarios—See the couple happily holding hands across the table, their rings sparkling in the candlelight? They're married, but not to each other.

"Not everything needs to be a thing," she said.

"Still . . ."

The author did signings and library events around the country, and fans were always asking, "Where do you get your ideas?" He told them they came from living life; that every place he went, every person he met, and every conversation he had was material. Touring a mobile home park led to *Tin City*. Chatting with a retiree in a small town that had lost half of its population in five years became *The Last Kind Word*. Visiting the Andrew Wyeth Gallery in the Brandywine River Museum of Art in Pennsylvania inspired *Dead Man's Mistress*.

He began entertaining possibilities.

She's hiding, he told himself.

From whom?

One of the band members. They were friends and lovers, but circumstances conspired to keep them apart. Now she's back, and as soon as he's finished with the set, she'll step out and they'll reunite in a Hallmark movie moment.

How would you know? You don't even watch the Hallmark Channel.

How's this? She's hiding.

From whom?

One of the band members. They were friends and lovers, but he betrayed her by sleeping with her BFF. She left town. Now she's back, and as soon as he's finished with the set, she'll step out and shoot him.

Okay, not a Hallmark movie.

The author glanced at the bag the woman had set on the chair next to her. It was large enough to hold a gun, he decided.

He turned toward the theater critic. She refused to meet his eyes, concentrating on the band, instead.

The author sipped his bourbon and listened to the Jacks swinging on "La Vie En Rose." Music was his refuge. It's where he went to escape life's trials and tribulations. That and baseball. And hockey. Yet his mind kept turning toward the woman, who continued to stare at the back of the pillar, her legs crossed. A pretty woman, he told himself. Young. At least too young for him. He had determined long ago that it was best to lust only after women who were more or less in his own age group. Yet there was something about her. Something old.

The woman had ordered a bottle of white wine, which the waiter served in a silver ice bucket. She poured a generous amount into a tall glass, took a sip, closed her eyes, and leaned back in the chair, balancing the glass with both hands below her breasts.

She's hiding, he told himself.

From whom?

Her friends. No, the people she wanted to be her friends. Classmates from high school who bullied her and rejected her because she was overweight and unattractive and wore thick glasses and was lacking in social graces, except now she was slender and beautiful and LASIK surgery had fixed her eyes and . . .

The author shook the thought from his head. He didn't like that story—the idea that the woman would want to connect with the people who treated her like something you scrape off the bottom of your shoe with a stick. In his version, she would tell her tormentors to go "entertain" themselves in no uncertain terms. Or better yet, forget that they even existed, living well being the best revenge.

He drank more bourbon and listened to the music.

She's stalking someone, the author told himself. Nah. From what he knew about stalkers, research he did for a book, she might not want the vic to see her, but she would absolutely want to see him.

The empty area immediately behind the woman slowly filled with couples who didn't mind that they couldn't see the stage while they danced. A young woman with shoulder-length hair danced alone. She noticed the woman behind the pillar and cautiously moved to a position where she could see her face. Pleased by what she saw, she waited until the Jacks began a new song before approaching. The dancer tapped the woman on the shoulder, spoke into the woman's ear, and gestured at the dance area. The woman smiled brightly and shook her head. The dancer made an are-you-sure gesture. The woman continued to smile even as she shook her head again. The dancer shrugged, and the woman stared at the pillar some more.

She's shy, the author told himself. And gay. Only she isn't comfortable enough with her sexuality to come out. Yet at the same time, there's a woman that she adores who has decided to move on because she's tired of waiting for her love to be reciprocated. The woman isn't actually stalking her. She followed her to the club because . . . Because . . . Why would she do that? the author wondered.

The waiter returned to the table and asked if the couple wanted another round. The author said they did. The theater critic asked for a dessert menu. There were six items available. The critic narrowed the list to two possibilities even while lamenting how terribly fattening they must be. The author knew her habits as well as she knew his and waited for the inevitable question.

"I can't eat all of this by myself," the critic said. "Will you split it with me?"

"Sure."

"Which dessert do you want?"

"You decide."

When the waiter returned with the drinks, the theater critic ordered something called Dunsmore's Delight, apparently named for the husband of the club's owner.

"Good choice," the waiter said.

He was then distracted by the woman behind the pillar. He moved to her table and leaned close to hear her over the band. The woman gestured at the dessert menu open in front of her. The waiter stepped back, a quizzical expression on his face. She smiled brightly yet again—such a lovely smile, the author told himself—and said, "Yes, one of each," loud enough to be heard.

The waiter spread his arms wide in surrender and left.

He returned a few minutes later, carrying a large round tray topped with every dessert on the menu plus one. The waiter served a Dunsmore's Delight to the mystery author and the theater critic. Everything else was placed before the woman seated behind the pillar.

"Enjoy," he said.

The author and theater critic agreed that it was one of the best desserts that they had ever eaten. The woman seemed to enjoy all of her desserts as well, although she only took a few bites of each, not finishing any.

She's a food critic, the author told himself, who doesn't want to be recognized by the club's staff or patrons. Except, would she need to hide behind a pillar to accomplish that?

The woman dabbed her mouth with a napkin, grabbed her bag, and stood. She glanced at the author who was pretending that he hadn't been watching her for most of the evening.

"Don't let anyone steal my table," she said.

"Never."

The woman moved toward the back of the club; going to the restroom, the author decided.

She has Type 1 diabetes, and she came to the club alone so she could indulge herself just this once without getting that look from her family and friends. Now she's off to give herself a shot of insulin to offset all the sugar and alcohol she just consumed.

That doesn't explain why she's sitting behind a pillar, though.

"You know," the theater critic said, "you could just ask her."

So the author did, the moment she returned.

"I love live music," the woman said. "Especially jazz. But I think music should be heard and not necessarily seen. Does that make sense?"

Yes, the author decided. Yes, it does.

By then the Eastside Jacks were wrapping up their last set of the evening. The band leader praised the crowd for being such a good audience and thanked it for coming out; he said it was a great club in general and that the band looked forward to returning in a few months.

"We take requests and some of them are unusual," he said. "This one was more unusual than most because the young lady asked that this be the last song we play tonight. 'St. James Infirmary Blues.' We hope you enjoy it."

The author liked the tune even before the Jacks began to play it. He had always thought of "St. James Infirmary Blues" as the quintessential New Orleans funeral song. It began slowly, almost like a dirge, and he could picture mourners slowly carrying a coffin to the cemetery while a brass band played somber hymns. Yet once the coffin was placed into the grave, the mood would shift and the band would begin to swing. The funeral would become a celebration of a life well lived, and the author knew, just knew, that it was the woman behind the pillar who had requested it.

He stole yet another glance at her. She held her bag on her lap, her eyes closed, her head bowed as the band leader sang the lyrics.

I went down to St. James Infirmary,
Saw my baby there,
Stretched out on a long white table,
So cold, so sweet, so fair.

The woman reached inside her bag and removed a small vial. She set the bag on the chair, opened the vial, and poured the contents into her long stem wineglass.

"Miss?" the author said.

The woman swirled the wine in her glass and drank it down in one long pull.

"Miss? What are you doing?"

She set the glass on the table, leaned back in her chair, folded her hands over her chest, and closed her eyes.

"Miss!"

The author was shouting now, yet no one could hear him above the swinging brass band. Few people were aware of what was happening behind the pillar.

The woman was smiling when her body began to tremble. She slid off her chair. The author leapt off his seat and caught her before she fell to the floor. He cradled her in his arms. She opened her eyes and smiled at him.

"My hero," she said.

She closed her eyes.

Let her go, let her go, God bless her,
Wherever she may be . . .

The theater critic had been trained in first aid. She also leapt off her seat and went to the woman. She took her wrist between her fingers while at the same time, feeling for a pulse in the carotid artery. She pulled an eyelid up and searched for a response in the woman's pupils.

"She's gone," she said.

The music was reaching a crescendo.

"Why would she do that?" the mystery author asked.

The band finished playing and the audience rose to its feet and began applauding thunderously as if that was the answer.

DUNSMORE'S DELIGHT

Recipe courtesy of Mary Tjosvold, PhD, owner of Crooner's Lounge and Supper Club, Minneapolis, Minnesota

Ingredients

Margaret's Cake (see below)

30 strawberries, cleaned and sliced thin

2 cups hazelnuts, toasted and crushed

3 cups whole milk

1½ cups heavy whipping cream

8 egg yolks

½ cup granulated sugar

¼ cup cornstarch

2 teaspoons vanilla extract

Directions

Make one chocolate Margaret's Cake (see recipe below). Remove from pans and let cool. Cut into ½-inch cubes. Toast in oven at 350 degrees for 7–10 minutes or until the outside is a little crusty. Remove from oven and let cool to room temperature.

Combine the sugar and cornstarch in a mixing bowl. Gradually add egg yolks and whisk until combined.

Whisk milk and cream in a sauce pan and warm over medium heat until mixture reaches a simmer. Remove from heat. Add egg mixture to sauce pan in a slow even stream while whisking continuously until thoroughly combined. Add vanilla. Return sauce pan to medium heat; stir continuously until the custard thickens. Remove from heat. Transfer custard to a mixing bowl and place in refrigerator to cool.

Place a layer of Margaret's Cake into the bottom of a large wineglass. Arrange the sliced strawberries in an even layer on the sides of the glass and press them into place. Once it is cooled, add the custard to the top of the cake. Sprinkle a thin layer of hazelnuts over the top of the custard. Repeat the process until the wineglass is completely filled.

Refrigerate until ready to serve.

MARGARET'S CAKE

Ingredients

2 cups flour

2 cups sugar

2 teaspoons baking soda

½ teaspoon iodized salt

1 egg

1 cup canola oil

1 cup buttermilk

1 cup coffee, cooled

½ cup cocoa powder

Directions

Grease two 8-inch round cake pans with butter and dust with flour.

Mix together all of the dry ingredients in a large mixing bowl.

Mix together the egg, oil, buttermilk, and coffee in a separate bowl.

Combine the contents of the two bowls, mixing thoroughly.

Fill the round pans with the cake mixture. Bake at 350 degrees for 25–30 minutes or until toothpick comes out clean.

WINDOW DRESSING

By Joel Arnold

SHERIFF BILLY BARLEE picked a piece of glass out of the dead man's hair, held it up to the sun, and spat at the mud.

Of all the days for a death to happen in Mantorville, it had to happen on Billy's birthday. His wife, Amy, and twelve-year-old daughter, Kate, had baked a chocolate cake and pan-fried the redeyes he'd caught that morning. He'd been ready to take a bite of the fish when he heard a not-so-faraway scream. He stared at the forkful of flaky meat for a moment, stood up, knees creaking, and strode to the front door. A small group gathered around something on the muddy road a block away outside the Hubbell House Hotel and Restaurant. As he walked toward the group, he saw the body. Another step and he saw the broken window.

"Anyone see what happened?" he asked the gathered townsfolk.

"He jumped out that window," Rita Mae Schoenstadt, a waitress at the Hubbell House, pointed to the broken third-story window of the hotel.

"I know what window he came out of," Billy said, turning to Rita Mae. She'd been a looker back in her day, and when he squinted, he could almost make out the woman she once was. "You seen him jump? Or was he pushed?"

Rita Mae opened her mouth, then shut it. Opened it and shut it again.

"You got something to say?" Billy asked.

"I was thinking," Rita Mae said.

"How about thinking out loud so I can hear you?"

"I'm not really positive one way or the other."

Rita Mae had always been a nervous woman. Quiet. Her husband, Dwight, owned the barbershop in town and talked enough for the both of them. He was fair at cutting hair, but his constant gossip of others rubbed Billy the wrong way.

He looked back up at the third story, then turned to the onlookers. "Anyone see what happened? Anyone at all?"

If someone saw the man jump, that could be the end of the matter, Doc Clayton could take over, and he'd get back to his fish and cake. Besides, he'd been hoping to end the 1890s without a murder this last half of the year.

He didn't recognize the dead man. Not from Dodge County and certainly not from Mantorville. "Anyone know him?" Billy asked.

The hotel's desk clerk and bartender, Jack Connelly, raised a hand. "He's from outta town. Out east somewhere. One of the stagecoach drivers. Checked in a few hours ago."

"Anything seem unusual about him?"

"Not that I noticed."

Billy leaned toward Jack and lowered his voice. "You been drinking?"

"Just the usual." Jack's usual was a tin cup full of whiskey he kept behind the bar.

"That all?"

"I might've had a coupla extra sips after I heard the commotion."

Billy sighed. One of his two deputies was down in Rochester getting married, while the other deputy was attending to an incident a few miles away in Kasson.

Seven-year-old Molly Gergens poked at the body with a stick. "Stop that!" Billy said, kicking a thick splash of mud at her. Then he asked, "Anyone see him jump? Anyone see him pushed?"

Rita Mae Shoenstadt opened her mouth as if to say something again, and again closed it. Billy ignored her. He wanted to get inside and go up to the room, but he needed to wait until Doc Clayton got here to watch after the body and give it a look-see.

He felt a tap on his shoulder. Billy turned around. Doc Clayton stood behind him. Finally, a wish come true. "You're quieter than a roasted turkey," Billy said. He nodded at the corpse, then nodded up at the third floor of the hotel. "All we know is that he came from up there, and now he's down here, dead as dirt. You might wanna peal him up outta the mud before the sun dries him in there. See if he has any other injuries."

Doc nodded and, without saying a word, knelt in the mud and examined the stagecoach driver.

"You," Sheriff Billy said, pointing at the inebriated desk clerk. "I need to see the guest register. Then I need to see his room."

· · · · ·

The deceased man had registered under the name Joseph Wilbanks and was allotted room 304. Billy climbed the two flights of stairs while Jack Connelly followed behind carrying the key in one hand and holding tightly onto the railing with the other, the extra sips of whiskey doing a number on his balance. Billy waited at the victim's door until Jack caught up. Jack's face was paler than when they started up the steps.

"Are you gonna be sick on me?" Billy asked.

Jack took a deep breath, exhaled, and shook his head. He was about to say something but then promptly fell to his knees and vomited on Billy's boots. Billy rolled his eyes. Nothing to do but grab the key from Jack's shaking hand and wipe his boots on Jack's trousers. "I'll let myself in," he said.

The room was small. A bed, a dresser with a washbasin on it, a porcelain pitcher full of water. A mirror hung on one wall between two paintings of hunting dogs, and there was a table adorned with two wooden chairs. On the floor was a duffel bag, and on the table was an ashtray with the last knuckle of a cigar hanging precariously on the lip. Next to the ashtray was a plate containing a T-bone steak and baked potato. The steak had a bite cut from it, and the bite rested within the tines of a silver fork. Billy picked up the fork, examined it, sniffed the steak, and put it in his mouth. Mmm . . . he cut off another hunk and ate that too. Best not to let it go to waste, he thought as his stomach growled. Then he remembered the fish and the cake waiting for him back home.

He cut off another bite—medium rare—and shoved it in his mouth, chewing quickly and swallowing. Oh dear God, that's good. And who knew how long he'd be stuck on this case? Couldn't be solving crimes on an empty stomach. That was common sense.

Besides, Billy thought, *it's my birthday.*

He heard more retching outside the door.

He examined the broken window. Some blood decorated the shards of glass, but other than that, not much else he could see.

If I was going to throw myself out a window, Billy thought, I'd've finished that steak and potato first.

He cut off another bite. Nodded. No, sir, I would not leave that behind.

Also—if I was going to jump out a window, hoping to end it all, why here? Only three stories high left a chance of survival—left the chance of only breaking a leg and making life even *more* miserable.

He looked outside.

Doc Clayton walked away with the muddied body thrown over his shoulder. The onlookers followed as he lugged it to his doctor's office, located in a back room of his one-story house two blocks away. Molly Gergens stayed behind looking up at Billy. She gathered a pile of mud, formed it into a ball, and threw it. She had a good arm but not quite good enough. The mud slapped against the hotel's limestone façade. Billy grabbed the potato off the plate and threw it. Molly ducked just in time.

Well, ain't that something. Billy examined the window's ledge and noticed a few more drops of blood he'd missed on first examination, and when he looked up at the top of the window frame, saw a thicker spattering.

Billy backed away and poked his head out the door into the hallway. "Jack?"

Jack sat with his back up against the wall, moaning.

"Who brought the food up here?" Billy asked.

"Food?" Jack groaned. "Go ask the cooks."

• • • • •

There were three of them, and since the lunch rush was over, they sat in rickety wooden chairs behind the Hubbell House smoking cigarettes. In the middle of them was a large, old tree stump holding a tin can for the ashes. Billy knew them all, typically good fellas but with a penchant for hard drinking after they closed up in the evening.

"Joseph," Billy said acknowledging the smallest of the three. He wore an impressively unkempt orange beard, his bald head covered by a cap. "Do you know who sent the steak up to room 304?"

The corners of Joseph's eyes crinkled into a smile, and he pulled at his whiskers. "No, sir," he said. "I make the meals to order. I don't tell 'em where to go." He looked at his companions, Calvin Riggs and Leroy Vicksburg. "Same as them," he said.

"Is that right?" Billy asked the others.

They nodded. Calvin mumbled, "S'right."

"Did any of you cook a medium rare steak with a baked potato on the side?"

They nodded. "Several," they said.

This wasn't getting him anywhere.

"When someone wants a meal delivered," Billy asked, "who delivers it?"

Calvin Riggs spoke around his cigarette, the smoke accenting each syllable. "There ain't no one special who delivers it. Whoever's available at the time." He looked up at the sky, his eyes following his path of smoke. "The most likely to deliver a meal would be one of the wait staff, or maybe the bellhop or the desk clerk. Any one of them have brought up meals to the guests at one point or another. I guess it's usually the one standing around looking for something to do."

"So none of you brought food up to room 304?" Billy asked.

They shook their heads and went back to smoking.

$\bullet \ \bullet \ \bullet \ \bullet \ \bullet$

The dead man's body lay naked across Doc Clayton's dining room table. The doctor examined it through a magnifying glass. His wife, Ethel, stood to the side, fuming, tapping her foot, waiting for the whole thing to be over so she could set the table for supper.

"Anything?" Billy asked.

"The man was stabbed." Doc pointed at the man's throat. "See there?"

Billy leaned over the three tightly spaced holes in the man's neck. "With a fork?" He remembered the delicious piece of steak he'd slid from the tines with his lips. Now he wondered about the red juice that ran down his chin. "Could he have done it to himself?"

Doc squinted. "Why would someone stab themselves with a fork?"

Billy shrugged and walked slowly around the dining room table. He'd lived in Mantorville for twenty years and thought highly of its citizens as well as the rest of the folks in Dodge County. He'd known Doc Clayton for most of those years. The doc had delivered his son and daughter and helped his wife through a bad bout of pneumonia. He'd even set Billy's leg after a nasty break when his horse threw him into a pile of quarried limestone.

"Did the fork kill him?" Sheriff Billy asked.

"No," the doc said, raising his eyebrows. "No, the fall killed him. The fork . . . Well, I haven't figured what that's all about."

Billy got to the point. "Did he jump or was he assisted out of the window?"

Doc Clayton shrugged. "Either way, he's dead."

"Surely," Billy said, nodding at the corpse. With a "Ma'am" and a dip of his head to Mrs. Clayton, Billy took his leave.

After Billy questioned a few more citizens without garnering any pertinent information, he remembered the fish and cake waiting for him. It had been a few hours since being interrupted from his celebration, and there wasn't much else he could do right now, so he headed home. At the very least, he could give his wife an update on the events of the day. Maybe she'd relight the candles for him so he could properly blow them out and stuff his face with a slice of her delicious chocolate cake.

• • • • •

His daughter smiled at him as Amy carried the cake in from their small kitchen and placed it in front of the sheriff. The flames on the candles sputtered as the beeswax dripped onto the cake. "Make a wish, Papa," Kate said.

Billy wished his deputy would get back from Kasson so that he could take over for the rest of the day. He blew out the candles. Amy pulled them from the cake, and Kate cut into it. She placed slices onto plates and handed one to her father. "Happy birthday, Papa."

"Thank you," he said. He winked at his wife. "How old am I?"

"Thirty-seven," Kate said.

"That old? Impossible."

"You act like you're sixty," Amy said.

Their laughter was cut short when a timid knock sounded on the door.

Kate pushed away from the table. "I'll get it."

Billy said, "No, I'll get it. Might be something to do with the killing."

He glanced at his untouched cake slice before opening the door.

Rita Mae Shoenstadt stood at the threshold looking at her feet.

"Rita Mae?"

She looked up, her eyes wet with tears.

"Why don't you come on in?" Billy said. "Have a slice of cake with us."

"Cake?" she asked.

"Chocolate," Billy said. "Amy made it."

"And I helped," Kate added.

"I guess I'll have a piece," Rita Mae said. "That is if you don't mind having a cold-blooded killer at your table."

· · · · ·

"You couldn't have pushed that fella out the window," Billy said, as they sat at the table enjoying the cake. Well, at least he and Amy and Kate were enjoying it.

"Might as well have," Rita Mae said.

Billy looked at his wife. "Maybe you and Kate should skedaddle for a bit. Mrs. Shoenstadt might not be comfortable talking in front of everyone."

"But Papa," Kate said.

Amy put a hand on her shoulder. "Come on. Let's take a walk."

Once they were out of earshot, Rita Mae leaned forward. "I'm an evil, evil woman."

Billy smiled. "Come on, Rita. It can't be all that bad. Tell me what's on your mind."

She slowly chewed a bite of cake.

"Rita?"

Finally, she set down her fork and looked up at him. She opened her mouth.

Then shut it.

She opened her mouth again.

Before she could close it again, another knock sounded on the door, this one hard and heavy.

Sheriff Billy rolled his eyes, pushed away from the table, and lumbered to the door as the knocking persisted. "Hold *on*," he said.

When he opened the door, he took a step back. Rita Mae's husband, Dwight, filled the doorway. He held a revolver.

"Where's Rita?" he bellowed.

"Before you take one step forward, you better aim that gun at the floor," Billy said.

Dwight ignored him and stepped inside. He saw his wife sitting at the table. "Rita? I been looking all over for you."

"It's over, Dwight," she said, her voice cracking with the effort.

"It ain't over 'til I say it is!"

Sheriff Billy thought of the steak and the fish and the cake and then thought of the gun and the weight of the man standing before him. He sighed once more before resigning himself to take the chance he needed to take. "Dwight!" he shouted, and when the man turned his attention again to the sheriff, Billy grabbed the man's gun and kneed him in the groin.

Dwight fell to his knees and bellowed, "No fair!"

Billy pointed the gun at Dwight's chest and stepped back out of reach. He turned to Rita. "You wanna explain what's going on?"

Rita stood up from the table and walked to Dwight.

Billy said, "Rita, you be careful!"

It was Rita's turn to roll *her* eyes. She kneeled next to Dwight and put her arms around him. At least as much of him as she could.

"You fool," she said to Dwight. "You darn fool!"

Billy sighed. He opened his mouth, but this time, Rita shushed him.

"Listen here, Sheriff. Dwight had no ill intent. Well, not unjustified, anyway. He just had a wrong notion and was trying to make things right."

"What kind of—*notion*—did Dwight have?" Billy asked.

"He had the notion that the man in room 304 was seducing me."

Billy's jaw dropped, realized that might look rude, and snapped his mouth shut. "Pray tell," he said.

Dwight said, "But you went up to his room."

"I was taking a meal to him. He wasn't feeling well and asked if we could cook him a steak and potato and take it to him in his room."

Dwight's jaw worked, moving side to side. "You mean—"

"Yes. I mean you killed the man for no good reason. You've heard of room service, haven't you?"

Dwight said, "You know we never stay at them fancy hotels. I just saw him talking to you all secret-like, then awhile later, you go on up to his room."

"He was ordering a steak and a baked potato!"

"Didn't look like you were writing any orders down. Ain't that what waitresses do?"

"You don't think I can't remember a simple order like that? You've known me all these years, and you think I can't *remember*?"

Billy looked from one to the other.

Dwight looked dumbfounded. Then his whole body collapsed into a sorry heap. "You saying I killed that man for nothing?"

Rita Mae nodded. Tears filled her eyes, but a smile stretched her lips wide. "I never thought you cared so much about me," she said.

Billy held up his hands. "Okay, okay, folks, I'm glad your undying love has been restored, but you do know that murder is frowned upon, right?"

Rita didn't seem to hear, planting kisses up and down her husband's neck and face.

"You do know you'll likely go to prison?"

The kissing continued. Billy asked, "Dwight, what about that fork? Did you stab him with the fork I found in his room?" Billy thought he already knew the answer, but was hoping he was wrong.

Dwight tried squirming out of Rita's grasp. He looked over at Billy. "I wiped it off on my shirt, cut off a hunk of steak, and stuck the fork in it. So it wouldn't look too *suspicious*."

Billy gulped.

A shadow appeared in the doorway.

What now?

"Sheriff?" It was his deputy, Brad Trainor, who'd been in Kasson most of the day. "Ain't it your birthday?"

Billy nodded. "Sure is. Now if you could escort this blubbering gentleman to the jail for me, I'd appreciate it. Oh, and stop by later tonight for a slice of Amy's chocolate cake."

• • • • •

An hour later, Billy, Amy, and Kate sat around a table at the Hubbell House Hotel's dining room. The fish he'd caught that morning had lost its luster, and he'd thought, *It's my birthday, so why not celebrate in style?*

A waiter set their plates in front of them. All three had ordered the steak and a baked potato. Kate and Amy liked theirs medium, while Billy preferred his medium rare. He sliced into it, stabbed the freshly shorn piece onto his three-tined fork. He placed it slowly in his mouth, savoring the tenderness and the juice that squirted into his mouth. He decided he liked his steak even better when it didn't come from the fork of a dead man.

TORTINO DI CIOCCOLATO
(HOT CHOCOLATE "LOVE" CAKE)

Recipe courtesy of Chef Vincenzo Giangiordano, Ristorante La Porta del Chianti, San Gusme, Italy. Recipe from the book Love in a Tuscan Kitchen: Savoring Life Through the Romance, Recipes, and Traditions of Italy *by Sheryl Ness*

Ingredients

6 ounces dark chocolate, chopped (use 60–70 percent chocolate)

10 tablespoons unsalted butter

3 large eggs

½ cup sugar

½ cup all-purpose flour

1 tablespoon cocoa powder

1 teaspoon baking powder

½ teaspoon salt

Directions

Preheat oven to 375 degrees.

Melt together the butter and chocolate in bowl over a water bath. You can create a water bath by placing a glass or metal bowl above a medium saucepan filled with water (half full). Warm the water over medium heat. The water should not be touching the bottom of the bowl. Set aside the melted chocolate to cool slightly. You can also use the microwave on 50 percent power for 1 to 2 minutes to melt the chocolate and butter together in a glass bowl.

Beat the eggs and sugar together well with a hand or stand mixer on medium until the mixture is creamy and light yellow—around 3 to 4 minutes. Slowly add the melted chocolate mixture (a little at a time) to the egg/sugar mixture.

Next add the dry ingredients: flour, cocoa powder, baking powder, and salt. Mix by hand with a whisk for 1 to 2 minutes until the mixture is smooth.

Spray 10 individual ramekins (4- to 6-ounce size) with spray oil or coat the inside well with butter. Pour the chocolate mixture into the ramekins, filling about ¾ full.

Bake cakes at 375 degrees for 10 to 12 minutes (it's better to undercook than overcook these, the middle should remain a bit melted). Turn the ramekins upside down on a small plate to turn out each individual cake. Serve warm with vanilla ice cream and berries.

Makes 8–10 cakes.

Soup du Jour:

Cemetery Soup in Bone broth

WHAT COOKS DO

A Culinary Essay by Erica Christ

MY HUSBAND AND I recently watched a documentary about an effort to recreate a 12-course meal from the 1890s, based on a recipe book from that time. The intent was to do everything as close to period perfect as possible—stove, methods, ingredients, even place settings.

It was interesting to see how much of a difference time makes. Many of the recipes that were chosen required days to properly prepare. If you don't rule anything out based on how long it takes to make, you can really do some interesting stuff. For example, you can make your own gelatin from cow hooves. You can make your own food coloring from beets and spinach. Then you can make multicolored jellies with fruit juice, the gelatin, and the coloring by adding one layer at a time and letting each layer set up before you add the next one. I'm curious enough that I would try to do something like that. I would try it once. Because it would drive me crazy. I'm curious, but not that patient.

In great contrast to the slow, painstaking preparation, of which the jellies were just one example, the actual service of the twelve-course meal needed to be timed to the minute. So, in addition to the rather large kitchen staff, there had to be a chief of service, and a service staff to carry the plates up and down three flights of stairs. There couldn't be more than three or four minutes between courses, and there were all sorts of other arcane Victorian dining rules to follow as well.

The food itself looked delicious and, since my family's business is a kind of old-fashioned German restaurant, neither the recipes nor the techniques were entirely unfamiliar to me. They were fancier and more extravagant than anything we would do at the restaurant. But we do make stocks and gravy from scratch and we make Austro-Hungarian Empire-style desserts. I understand that most people do not. Finding a calf's head for mock turtle soup was one of the challenges highlighted in the documentary. I was surprised by this because it wouldn't be hard for us. We get whole veal calves in once a month or so and my Dad butchers them down into schnitzels and uses the trim, or extra, for bratwurst. Speaking of animal heads, last summer, for the 500th anniversary of the Reinheitsgebot (the German beer purity law), we had a medieval-inspired meal at the restaurant, with beer pairings for each course. One of the seven courses was a whole, roasted pig. It was supposed to be a suckling pig, which top out at twenty or thirty pounds. My dad thought that sounded pointlessly tiny, and, since you pay a lot more per pound the smaller you go, he went with a bigger, cheaper pig. We still snicker to each other about the shrieks from unsuspecting serving staff going into the cooler for ketchup and coming face to face with a grimacing, brainless head on a 120-pound dead pig.

The recipes that were prepared in the documentary made it clear that, in general, there was a much wider variety of groceries available in the 1890s than there is today. That's in general, as in, to the regular grocery shopper. However, it is true that there are fish that have been fished out now; there is an endangered species act and much stricter rules about game and how and where it's sold; and there are changes in taste that have resulted in some foods, such as horse meat, being taken off the market.

We are living in the age of convenience. We, as a society don't make things from scratch, as a rule. You can buy whole wheat berries and rye berries to grind your own flour, but you have little choice but the one wheat berry that your co-op sells. You don't get to choose which wheat you want or need for your flour. Still, most people don't make their own bread, much less grind their own flour. Once upon a time, bakers did get to choose which wheat berries they wanted, and which grind of which flour. And they made their own bread and cakes and pastries. Everyone did. And now we don't. Developers are building apartments now without kitchens, for crying out loud.

I make bread from scratch. I make yogurt and jam and soup. Sure, I don't make my own gelatin and food coloring, but like I said, I would try it once. So, this documentary really spoke to me. It was fascinating to see what it is like if you go beyond the recipes and actually cook and serve as they did 120 ago.

The documentary took place in a Victorian brownstone. For it, a wood-fired, cast iron stove and masonry oven were brought in. One of the courses was slices of saddle of venison. Apparently, the best way to cook saddle of venison is at more than 500 degrees and in a masonry oven. It doesn't take much to imagine how easy it would be to burn yourself badly with one false move not to mention how hot it would be working in the kitchen of a Victorian brownstone with a cast iron oven wood fired to 500 degrees. It's hot in *my* kitchen in the winter with the electric oven turned up to 450 degrees. But with a glowing, radiating, hot box like those in Victorian kitchens, even in the dead of winter, you'd be sweating up a storm. In the summer it would be inhumane.

In fact, as the kitchen staff prepared the ultimate meal, the film showed quite clearly how physically demanding it was: how hot it was, how heavy the pots filled with stock and meat were, how much cooks had to hustle to get things timed correctly, and how quickly cooks had to adjust if something didn't go exactly as planned. If you have any experience at all with the production end of anything, you could see how magnificently focused these cooks were. If you don't have that experience, it would look chaotic and, frankly, unpleasant and dangerous. In the end, all twelve plates of all twelve courses went out on time and each plate looked beautiful.

And then, the kitchen staff all went upstairs to the dining room to receive the applause of the twelve guests. It should have been a nice moment, and maybe, in reality, it was, but it made me unbearably sad. It was just *so* much work and a little polite applause isn't much acknowledgment, all things considered. In fact, it was so much work that nothing anyone could say or do could possibly be grateful or admiring enough, in my opinion. I'm missing the point and I know that. The point was just to do it. The rewards were intrinsic; plus, they all got paid, and they're immortalized on film. I'm sure everyone was happy they were involved in the project. It was a great challenge and they succeeded in accomplishing their goal. The twelve guests were all food people themselves: chefs, cookbook authors, food writers. If anyone could appreciate such a meal, they could.

Nonetheless. It isn't just about appreciating it. In the real world, all through history, anywhere around the globe, the people for whom such a feast is prepared are never, ever, *ever* the people who could or would *prepare* such a feast. All that skill, that finesse and knowledge, and all those hours; all the sweat and self-discipline; all that magic is, and has been, almost always in service of a class of people who, while they may work, they do not do manual work; they do not do work that demands equal parts dexterity, knowledge, stamina, and taste. The work of cooking and serving food is not held in high esteem in our society. The people with the money to pay for the best food, very often have little regard for those that provide them with their haute cuisine. They are, often, just plain assholes. They may very well be assholes who know good food when they taste it, but they are nonetheless assholes.

The Sacher torte was first made by a young baker's apprentice in the kitchen of Prince von Metternich. The story goes that Metternich had some guests he particularly wanted to impress, which meant serving something with a lot of chocolate in it, a rare ingredient in late-eighteenth century Vienna. The baker was sick, so the job fell to his sixteen-year-old apprentice. He was told that failure was not an option. Because Metternich was an asshole. And young Franz Sacher succeeded, with what is now known as the Sacher torte.

At least Franz Sacher got to have his creation named after him. The dish known as Beef Stroganoff was named after the Stroganovs, a Russian noble family. The name of the chef who created it for them has been lost to history. The Stroganovs, it should be noted, were assholes.

I could give you a hundred more examples. The culinary arts that transform the ingredients we think of as basic, into a food that looks, tastes and smells like something entirely different, are a set of skills, knowledge and judgment that include chemistry, inventiveness, and exquisitely fine-tuned senses. Where would our cuisine be without all the people who figured out what is possible with an egg? What fun would eating be for us now without the experience of all the people who poisoned themselves eating mushrooms, who vomited out spoiled meat, and who looked at every plant and animal they saw and wondered if it would be good to eat and how best to cook it? We should be grateful beyond measure to all the chefs, cooks, and bakers who came before us and those we have now in our lives.

I suppose I could say we should also be grateful that rich people have employed cooks for at least two thousand years, giving cooks the space and resources to make all the discoveries and innovations we enjoy now. But it's hard for me to set aside the disproportionately unfair economic aspect of that history; the dismal pay and circumstances that often characterized that employment. Even in the documentary that I described, it would be a safe bet to say that the people who painstakingly layered the molded jellies, the ones who carefully ladled out scalding hot soup, and those that delicately assembled each plate of each course received fair compensation but not as high as the compensation for the person who organized the dinner, nor did it compare well to the income level of the dinner guests.

I don't wonder why people choose to be cooks. Everybody has to do something. I do wonder why people, cooks and otherwise, do things that are beyond all expectation, beyond ordinary measure, and, frankly, heroic under the circumstances? Why do something so unreasonably challenging that no price high enough can be charged for it? Why sacrifice so much of yourself that there's not enough gratitude in the world to acknowledge it? It happens all the time, all around us.

There is in food, as there is in art, an intrinsic generosity. So many cooks go beyond feeding people, beyond nourishing people, to delighting people and transporting them. It's too much to comprehend why someone would do it, and it's much too limiting to think that they do it for their boss or patron or any small group of people. It is truly beyond reason and therefore it must be enough to simply say, they do it. They should be paid more, and they do it. They do things that enrich our lives more than we even know how to acknowledge, and they do it. They endure scorn. They risk injury. They do it. They do it. They do it.

What, then, can we do? We cannot be grateful enough or pay enough. I don't know about you, but I can't afford to pay what a good meal is worth to me, just as I can't afford to pay what a house full of art is worth to me. And yet, I get to eat good meals. I have a house full of art. How can I balance that equation?

What I can do, what we can all do, is be generous. We can, indeed we must, be as generous as often and as widely as possible. It is the only way to balance that equation. It is how we can repay otherwise unpayable debts.

LIVER DUMPLING SOUP

Recipe from Erich Christ, who has owned and cooked at The Black Forest Inn in Minneapolis, Minnesota, since 1965

Ingredients

1 pound ground beef

½ pound onion, diced

½ pound liver, chopped fine

2 each eggs

1 tablespoon salt

2 teaspoons pepper

¾ cup bread crumbs

1½ gallons beef stock

2 each bay leaf

2 tablespoons basil

Salt and pepper

Directions

Grind or mix together beef, onion, liver, eggs, salt, pepper, and bread crumbs.

Form into 2-ounce meatballs.

Heat the beef stock, bay leaf, basil, salt, and pepper to a boil.

Place the meatballs in the stock and simmer until done (45 minutes).

Yield: 10–12 generous servings

ABOUT THE AUTHORS

MARCIA ADAIR spent her childhood reading mysteries by flashlight under the covers. By the time adulthood rolled around, she had earned a master's degree in journalism and launched her career as a professional writer and editor. Her short stories appear in anthologies, including *Dark Side of the Loon* (2018) and *Minnesota Not So Nice: Eighteen Tales of Bad Behavior* (2020), from the Twin Cities Chapter of Sisters in Crime, and *Malice Domestic 14: Mystery Most Edible* (2019). She received the 2018 Dorothy Cannell Scholarship. She is a member of Sisters in Crime. Visit her author page at www.facebook.com/MarciaAdairAuthor/.

JOEL ARNOLD's writing has appeared in dozens of magazines and anthologies, and his short story collection *A Wrinkle in Crime: 10 Stories of Foul Play, Murder & Revenge* contains even more mystery and crime fiction. He lives in Savage, Minnesota.

M.E. BAKOS is the author of *Fatal Flip* and *Deadly Flip* in her Home Renovator Mysteries series. If you liked "Champagne Wishes and Caviar Dreams," you can follow house-flipping fun with the same characters in her series. Her short stories have appeared in Sisters in Crime anthologies and national women's magazines. She lives in Minneapolis, Minnesota, with her husband, Joe Sebesta, and their spoiled morkie. She is a member Twin Cities Sisters in Crime, Sisters in Crime National Chapter, and the Guppies. Visit her website at mebakos.wixsite.com/author.

ERICA CHRIST is a writer, playwright, and the artistic director of Cheap Theatre. She also works at her family's business, the Black Forest Inn. She lives with her husband and dog in the Whittier neighborhood of Minneapolis, Minnesota.

A past president of the Private Eye Writers of America (PWA), DAVID HOUSEWRIGHT has earned an Edgar Award from the Mystery Writers of America, a Shamus nomination from PWA, and three Minnesota Books Awards for his Rushmore McKenzie and Holland Taylor detective novels as well as other tales of murder and mayhem in the Midwest. He has also written numerous short stories for various anthologies including *Full House* (Down and Out Books) and publications as diverse as *Ellery Queen Mystery Magazine* and *True Romance*. His name and face were recently added to "Minnesota Writers on the Map" by the Minnesota Historical Society and Friends of the St. Paul Public Library. David's twenty-fourth novel—*From The Grave*—will be published in 2020 (St. Martin's Minotaur). Visit his website at www.davidhousewright.com.

CHRIS NORBURY is the award-winning author of the mystery-suspense-thrillers *Straight River* and *Castle Danger*, featuring Matt Lanier, a southern Minnesota farm kid turned professional musician whose middle-class world is turned upside down when he uncovers a conspiracy run by a powerful real estate magnate. Chris is a member of both the Twin Cities and national chapters of Sisters in Crime and the Alliance of Independent Authors (ALLi). His essays on wilderness canoeing have been published in the *Boundary Waters Journal*. A volunteer Big Brother since 2000, Chris donates a portion of his book sales to Big Brothers Big Sisters of Southern Minnesota. During golf season, he works on perfecting his golf game and makes time to canoe the Boundary Waters Canoe Area Wilderness. He and his wife live in Owatonna, Minnesota. Visit his website at chrisnorbury.com.

AMY PENDINO is a Minnesota native. A former middle school teacher, she now spends her days with horses, coffee, and books. She's a member of the Twin Cities chapter of Sisters in Crime. *The Witness Tree*, her debut novel, won three indie writing awards; her poetry has been published in regional anthologies, magazines, and reviews. Visit her website at www.amypendino.com.

DIANE SISMOUR has written poetry and fiction for more than thirty-five years in multiple genres. She lives with her husband in eastern Pennsylvania at the foothills of the Blue Mountains. Diane is a member of Romance Writers of America, Bethlehem Writer's Group LLC, Horror Writers Association, and Liberty States Fiction Writers. Visit her website at www.dianesismour.com.

JEANNE SHIELDS grew up in a suburb of Minneapolis. She has wonderful memories of her childhood summers, reading mysteries that had been gathered from the bookmobile and read in the neighbor's screened-in porch. She became totally consumed by the genre, however, during college when a couple of classmates sat discussing why one single event in the lives of writers sometimes changed the course of their writing careers from literary to mystery and suspense. Jeanne has a short story published in the Twin Cities Sisters in Crime anthology, *Festival of Crime*.

KATHLEEN TAYLOR is the author of hundreds of craft magazine articles, six Tory Bauer mysteries, five knitting books, three coloring books, one mainstream novel, and, now, forty years into her career, one short story. She lives in South Dakota.

CHERYL ULLYOT retired from Northwest Airlines in 2008 after thirty-nine years of service as a flight attendant. An avid mystery reader, she has turned to mystery writing in her retirement. She is a member of Mystery Writers of America, Sisters in Crime, and a supportive writing group. She has been published in *Hennepin History* and *Contrails* magazines. Two of her short stories appeared in the Twin Cities Sisters in Crime anthologies, *Festival of Crime* and *Dark Side of the Loon*.

RENEE VALOIS is co-author of *The Devil and the Diva*, which was a nominee for a Minnesota Book Award in genre fiction. *Minnesota Monthly* magazine also named it one of the five best books of the year in their "Best of the Cities" issue. A National Endowment for the Arts Fellow in theater and musical theater, Renee regularly writes theater reviews for the *St. Paul Pioneer Press*. She has been a contributing writer for *History Channel Magazine,* and her fiction and poetry have appeared in literary magazines. She has also written award-winning commercials, videos, and advertising for clients such as McDonald's, Harley Davidson, Mall of America, Levi's, and Target. She is copy director at Aveda.

JASON LEE WILLIS is an author who teaches high school English, indigenous studies, creative writing, and mythology. He has published several books, including his newest series, the Dream Catcher Chronicles, set in central Minnesota. Jason grew up in South Dakota and currently lives in Minnesota, where he lives the life of a hobbit by gardening, writing, walking around barefoot, wearing vests, fishing, and going on adventures with his wife, Julie.

ABOUT THE EDITOR

RHONDA GILLILAND was voted Best Home Cook of October 1998 by the *St. Paul Pioneer Press*. She co-edited *Cooked to Death: Tales of Crime and Cookery* and is editor of the Cooked to Death series. *Volume III: Hell for the Holidays* was a finalist for the Killer Nashville Silver Falchion Award. She wrote, produced, and directed the award-winning *Come and Get Your Love*, a Native American thriller. She is a member of Twin Cities Sisters in Crime and served as president 2012–2015. She is a member of the Mystery Writers of America and a Yelper since 2008. A Saint Paul, Minnesota resident, she lives with her husband, a Russian Orthodox deacon, and a tabby named Stryper.

Made in the USA
Monee, IL
25 February 2020